"THE CHICKEN AND DUMPLINGS WERE THE BEST I've ever eaten, Shade," Maggie said. "You and your mother's recipe deserve all the credit. Thanks," she murmured shyly, then kissed him quickly on the cheek.

He gave her a devlish grin. "Is that little peck all I get for slaving over a hot stove for hours? Come on, you can do better than that."

He gathered her in his arms and brought his face close to hers. Her eyes closed automatically. She waited. He didn't kiss her. Her eyes opened. "What are you waiting for?"

"For you."

Damn him for making her take the responsibility! She almost pulled away and left him standing there with that smug look on his face. Then she thought, *I'll show you buster!* She planted a fervent, open-mouthed kiss on him designed to melt his boot heels.

Her plan backfired. From the moment their lips met and his tongue plunged into ther mouth, she was the one who went up in flames. . . .

WHAT ARE *LOVESWEPT* ROMANCES?

They are stories of true romance and touching emotion. We believe those two very important ingredients are constants in our highly sensual and very believable stories in the LOVESWEPT line. Our goal is to give you, the reader, stories of consistently high quality that may sometimes make you laugh, sometimes make you cry, but are always fresh and creative and contain many delightful surprises within their pages.

Most romance fans read an enormous number of books. Those they truly love, they keep. Others may be traded with friends and soon forgotten. We hope that each LOVESWEPT romance will be a treasure—a "keeper." We will always try to publish

LOVE STORIES YOU'LL NEVER FORGET
BY AUTHORS YOU'LL ALWAYS REMEMBER

The Editors

Loveswept ® 667

SLIGHTLY SHADY

JAN HUDSON

BANTAM BOOKS
NEW YORK · TORONTO · LONDON · SYDNEY · AUCKLAND

SLIGHTLY SHADY

A Bantam Book / February 1994

*LOVESWEPT and the wave design are registered
trademarks of Bantam Books, a division of
Bantam Doubleday Dell Publishing Group, Inc.
Registered in U.S. Patent
and Trademark Office and elsewhere.*

*If you would be interested in receiving protective vinyl covers for your
Loveswept books, please write to this address for information:*

*Loveswept
Bantam Books
P.O. Box 985
Hicksville, NY 11802*

ISBN 0-553-44091-8

Published simultaneously in the United States and Canada

*Bantam Books are published by Bantam Books, a division of Bantam Dou-
bleday Dell Publishing Group, Inc. Its trademark, consisting of the words
"Bantam Books" and the portrayal of a rooster, is Registered in U.S. Patent
and Trademark Office and in other countries. Marca Registrada. Bantam
Books, 1540 Broadway, New York, New York 10036.*

PRINTED IN THE UNITED STATES OF AMERICA

OPM   0 9 8 7 6 5 4 3 2 1

For Lori

PROLOGUE

On Monday after Thanksgiving, the morning of his fortieth birthday, Paul Berringer awoke at six-fifteen as usual. He worked out for thirty-five minutes in the fully equipped gym in his basement, swam ten laps in the indoor pool, showered, shaved, dressed in an Armani suit, and was at the breakfast table by a quarter to eight.

His housekeeper served him Monday's one poached egg, two slices of crisp bacon, and one piece of whole wheat toast on Spode china, and eight ounces of orange juice in a Waterford crystal glass. While he ate, he read the *Dallas Morning News*. His meal finished, he poured a cup of decaffeinated coffee from a silver pot and read the *Wall Street Journal*. With a second cup of coffee, he scanned the *New York Times*.

At a quarter to nine, he drove his black Ferrari to his office in downtown Dallas and rode up the private elevator to his penthouse domain. He nodded to Mrs. Harris, his executive assistant for the past eight years, and walked through the door to his hand-carved mahogany desk. He sat down in his high-backed leather chair, unpacked his briefcase, and picked up a pen.

He didn't write. For some reason he couldn't. Tossing down the gold pen, he swiveled his chair around to look out the window at the Dallas skyline.

He'd never felt so empty in his life. Hollow to the bone.

For several minutes he simply sat and watched a sparrow on the ledge outside. In many ways he envied that small brown bird. Its life was basic. It ate. It slept. It flew. It didn't give a tinker's damn about long-range planning, ulcers, profit margins, or social amenities.

He sucked in a deep breath, clenched his teeth resolutely, and swiveled back around. Picking up the pen again, he tried to sign the top letter on the stack of correspondence Mrs. Harris had left on the corner of his desk. His hand rebelled.

He tried again. His hand, which had worked perfectly well for forty years, refused to cooperate.

"To hell with the whole damned mess!" he said in disgust, flinging the pen across the room.

He sprang from his chair, grabbed his empty briefcase, strode out of his office, and stopped at Mrs. Harris's desk. "Get in touch with my mother, my brothers, and Jack Rule. Tell them that they're going to have to run things for a while. I'm leaving."

"But—but," she sputtered, "where are you going?"

"Away."

Mrs. Harris looked alarmed. "When will you return?"

"I don't know. Maybe never. Tell them I'll be in touch in about six months."

ONE

Maggie Marino's car jolted over another pothole in the road that tunneled through the thick woods. The springs of the ten-year-old station wagon she'd bought before she left New York couldn't take much more. The blasted thing had to last awhile longer; all her worldly possessions were crammed into it. She prayed that the hard drive of her computer wasn't shot to hell from the battering of this godforsaken Texas cow path.

Byline, the scruffy-looking tom cat who'd adopted her last year, set up a howl inside his carrying case on the front seat.

"Hang on, fella. It can't be much farther. The lawyer said it was two point four miles from the cutoff at Big Buck's." She glanced at the odometer, then remembered that it had stopped working in Arkansas.

The lawyer had given her warnings along with those directions. Her uncle's river house was simple and remote, he'd told her. Maggie didn't care. With no job, no prospects, and a dwindling bank account, she couldn't be choosy. And anything was better than living with threatening phone calls and attempts on her life. Nobody would find her here. Until two weeks ago even *she* didn't know she had an Uncle Silas—dead or otherwise.

The rutted dirt road ended just ahead in a clearing of trees dense with spring growth. Finally, she'd arrived at her refuge. The tension of the past week abated.

As she spied the mailbox, the blossoming smile on her face faded. A desolate, sick feeling crept into her chest.

Where the cabin had stood were only a brick chimney and charred beams. She wanted to cry. Instead she beat her fist against the steering wheel. Maggie Marino hadn't shed a tear in over twenty years, and she wasn't about to start crying now. She was a scrapper, and she'd survived worse than this.

Byline yowled again.

"Just a damn minute," she told the cat. She went around to the other side of the station wagon and unlatched the door to the carrier. Byline hissed, then he was a mere gray streak spurting past her and into the underbrush. "Get lost and see if I care!" she yelled after him.

Hands on her hips, Maggie kicked aside an empty beer can and surveyed the burned-out remnants of the cabin. She could see the blackened remains of a refrigerator and a few other barely recognizable items. A rickety shed, with a flat-bottomed boat upended inside, had survived the fire, but the shed had only three walls. It certainly wasn't livable.

She rolled her eyes heavenward and sighed. "What next?"

A clap of thunder echoed over the muddy river.

Maggie trudged into Big Buck's, the disreputable-looking place at the cutoff that advertised beer, bait, and beds. Her sneakers were muddy; her jeans and shirt were sopping wet; her hair was plastered to her head; and she had cat scratches on both arms.

The long room she entered had a wooden floor and walls of aged, knotty pine liberally decorated with mounted deer heads and neon signs. Near the bar that stretched along one half of the back wall were several tables covered with red checkered plastic. An empty dance floor and a bandstand took up about a third of the rest of the place, which reeked of tobacco smoke and pine cleaner.

Maggie had thought she was alone until she heard the click of pool balls. She peered at the corner and saw a long-legged man leaning over a pool table, cue in hand, concentrating on his shot. She'd always been a sucker for a cute butt, and his faded jeans stretched over a taut, well-muscled derriere that was the most enticing one she'd ever encountered.

Reining in her inappropriate thoughts, she cleared her throat. "Excuse me." She ventured closer.

The man took his shot, then straightened. With one hand on his outslung hip, he leaned on his cue stick as if it were a staff and looked at her. She almost swallowed her gum. He was the sexiest thing she'd run across in her entire thirty-five years, two months, and four days. Broad-shouldered and slim-waisted, he must have been at least six feet six in his scruffy boots.

No midget herself, she adored tall men.

His tousled mop of thick black hair was faintly streaked with silver strands and curled well below the turned-up collar of his sleeveless jean jacket. He had a thick mustache and several days' growth of beard. Below the short sleeve stretched over his left bicep she could see the bottom part of an intricate tattoo.

Sexy, yes. But a bit menacing as well. His eyes, so pale a green that they seemed to glow in contrast to his deeply tanned skin, impaled her. Discomforted by his stare, her gaze dropped to the front of the ragged, olive-drab T-shirt he wore beneath the faded jacket. There was a hole ripped under the neck band and a tuft of dark hair poked through. That hole was mesmerizing.

Vaguely aware that he'd spoken, she said, "Pardon?" and glanced to his face again. She promptly swallowed her gum.

He was smiling. And saints in heaven what a smile! He had beautiful, perfect, white teeth, and deep dimples in his cheeks.

"I said, 'Look what the cat dragged in.'" His low-pitched voice resonated through her like the thrum of a bass fiddle.

Maggie's hand flew to her dripping hair. She must look a fright. "Well, the cat caused the problem, but I did the dragging. Are you Big Buck? I need some information."

"Nope. Buck's in the kitchen. I'll get him. And I'll rustle up a towel for you while I'm at it." He took a swig from a long-necked beer bottle, then ambled through a door at the end of the bar.

Awestruck, she watched his loose-limbed gait as he disappeared. He was better than

Tom Selleck and Sam Elliot rolled into one. She wondered what he was doing in a hick dive like this and hoped he didn't have the I.Q. of a green bean and the savvy of a leek.

The food metaphors reminded her of the gnawing in her stomach. She'd skipped lunch several hours ago.

The door by the bar opened, and another man entered. His gray hair stood up in a bristly flattop, and he wore a white bibbed apron with the strings tied around his middle. A massive man, he wasn't quite as tall as the pool player, but he made up in girth what he lacked in height. He walked toward her with a slight hitch in his gait and a friendly smile on his florid face.

"Shade said you needed this," he said, handing her a towel. "I'm Buck. Buck Faulkner. Hep ya?"

"Pardon?"

"Shade said you was lookin' for information."

"Oh. Yes. I'm Maggie Marino." She swiped the towel over her wet face and arms and tried to blot her hair. "Silas O'Connell was my uncle, and I inherited his property. But it seems that the house has burned."

Shade ambled back into the room and rested

his taut posterior on the top rung of a wooden chair back, balancing himself on his outspread feet and the pool cue he held between his long legs. A sad-eyed hound she hadn't noticed before roused himself from beneath the pool table, lumbered across the room, and settled himself at Shade's feet.

"Yep. Burnt last Saturday night."

Maggie's eyes seemed drawn to the hands wrapped around that stick. Big hands with long fingers and neatly trimmed nails. His thick thighs strained the fabric of his faded jeans. Jeans bleached almost white along the placket—

Horrified at the blatant path her gaze had taken, she glanced up quickly to Shade's face. A faint look of amusement played at one corner of his mouth. She glared at him, swearing silently that if he laughed, she'd snatch that pool cue from his hands and crown him.

She swung her attention back to Buck. "Pardon?"

As if he assumed she had a hearing problem, Buck said loudly, "Silas's place burnt last Saturday night. Must have been some damned fool kids. By the time we saw the fire, wasn't a thang we could do about it. Burnt slap down to the ground."

Maggie had been hoping against hope that she'd found the wrong house, that her uncle's cabin, her refuge, was still intact. She heaved a dejected sigh. "I was afraid you were going to say that."

"Sorry about Silas's passin' last summer. Known him most of my life. Didn't know he had any kin left, though I seem to remember him mentioning a sister once. I recall they had some kind of fallin'-out."

"My mother," Maggie said. "She died when I was ten, and I never knew that I had an uncle. The attorney finally located me only ten days ago."

"You don't talk like you come from around these parts," Buck said.

Maggie laughed. "No, I'm from New York."

"New York City? Well, I swan. You're a long way from home."

"That's for sure. Is there somewhere nearby where I could get a room and a meal? Cheap?"

"We got four empty cabins out back, and supper'll be ready in a few minutes. Twenty dollars a night without meals, thirty with."

Maggie did some mental arithmetic, frowned, and chewed the inside of her cheek. The price was more than reasonable, but her financial resources were extremely low. She'd virtually wiped out her savings last year when she'd bought the condo—which she'd been able to rent to cover her mortgage, thank God—and her paycheck had stopped the month before when her editor canned her. Buying the station wagon, clunker that it was, then having to overhaul its transmission in Tennessee and the fuel pump in Mississippi, plus the extra nights she'd had to spend in motels, had carved a big chunk from the meager amount left in her savings account. She'd counted on living rent free with food and incidentals as her only expenses until she could finish her article. The "incidentals" had gotten out of hand.

Shade sniffed the air and said, "Buck, what's that smell coming from the kitchen?"

"The potaters!" Buck hurried away, muttering. "If them golldurned things has scorched again, there'll be hell to pay."

Shade chuckled. "Buck's not much of a cook. His wife, Sybil, usually handles that part of the business, but she's in Shreveport helping their daughter who's just had her first baby. Want a beer?"

"I'd love a beer." Maggie sank down into one of the wooden chairs. Ignoring the clammy feeling of her clothes, she propped her elbows on the table, her chin against her fists, and tried to figure out what to do next. Even at thirty dollars a night, she couldn't survive long without a job.

"Here you go." Shade offered the bottle he held by the neck. She reached for it, but he continued to hold on, and his little finger slid down to stroke the valley between her thumb and forefinger. "Trouble?"

The soft rumble of his voice and the simple stroke of his finger brought a sudden rush of tears to her eyes. Silly, she thought, blinking. Maggie Marino didn't cry; she was too tough to go all weepy in the face of a little adversity.

"Thanks," she said, taking the beer. "Nothing I can't handle."

She took a big swig from the bottle, relishing the cool bite of the beer as it slid down her throat. She could handle anything that life threw at her. Hadn't she been surviving on her own since she was fifteen years old? Glancing up, she meant to tell him exactly that, but something in his soft green gaze stilled her tongue, a tongue long honed to razor sharpness. She had the strangest urge to throw herself into his arms and blurt out all her woes.

She didn't like the feeling; she didn't like it a damned bit.

Dragging her gaze from his, she squirmed in her seat and downed another swallow of beer. Twisting the bottle around, she focused her attention on the label, reading every word printed there.

She heard the scrape of his chair on the wooden floor. "Planning to stay around here for long?" he asked, sitting directly across from her now.

Maggie didn't look up from the label. She didn't dare. She shrugged. "Since the house burned, I don't know. I suppose I'll decide after I talk to the attorney."

"Potaters ain't too bad," Buck said, rejoining them. "Pour a little gravy over 'em and you'll never know the difference."

"Can you cook?" Shade asked Maggie.

"Of course I can cook," she said. Hadn't she spent nine miserable months as food editor of that rag she'd worked on after she graduated from college?

"Buck's been trying to hire someone to cook," Shade said.

"I have?" Buck cleared his throat. "I mean, I have."

"Buck and I aren't much on cooking," Shade said. "If the right person came along, I expect that it would be worth room and board to have decent meals around here, wouldn't it, Buck?"

"Sure would. Might you be interested, li'l lady?" he asked.

She bristled. "My name is Maggie."

"Well, Miss Maggie, this would be temporary, you understand, till Sybil gets back in a few weeks."

She looked up sharply. "Are you serious?"

"Wouldn't have offered if I wasn't."

"What would be required?" she asked.

"Three meals a day, through the week," Buck said. "Got somebody that comes in special for the weekends when business picks up. Mostly it's just Shade and me around here to eat, but sometimes we get a couple of fishermen and such through the week who want to take supper. Sometimes another drop in or two. Nothin' fancy at noontime—homemade soup and sandwiches is what we generally have. Big meal's in the evenin'. And you'd have to buy the groceries. I hate pushing them danged fool carts around."

Maggie considered the offer. Taking a job as a cook was an odd thing for a woman who'd been a reporter on one of New York's largest newspapers, but at the moment it seemed like an answer to a prayer. She was desperate.

But not so desperate that she would jump at the first offer. That was never good business.

"I don't do mornings," she said.

Buck frowned. "Beg pardon?"

Shade chuckled, and the soft sound made her go warm all over. "Buck and I can probably handle breakfast, can't we, Buck?"

The heavy man scratched his bristly head. "I reckon so."

"Then you've got a deal, Mr. Faulkner." She stood and shook hands with him.

"Call me Buck. Shade, why don't you hep the li'l lady unload her stuff in number two." He retrieved a key from behind the bar and handed it to Maggie. "While you're getting settled, I'll rustle up the rest of our supper."

"Thanks, but I don't need any help. By the way," Maggie said. "I've got a cat."

Buck shrugged. "No problem. We've got mice."

The rain had slowed to a light drizzle. Maggie pulled the station wagon into the second of the carports that separated the line of six weathered-cedar units behind the beer hall. The Plaza it wasn't, but she'd be grateful if it had a bed and clean sheets. The porch flower boxes, planted with red geraniums, gave her some hope.

She unlocked the back of the wagon and grabbed a suitcase in each hand. As she turned she collided with a large body. She let out a yelp and dropped the bags. Her hand slapped her chest as if she'd been shot.

Shade steadied her by the shoulders. "You okay?"

"You scared me out of about ten years' growth."

He chuckled. "Looks to me like you already

have your full growth, Miss Maggie. How tall are you?"

She glared up at him and stuck out her chin. "My name is not Miss Maggie. It's Maggie or Ms. Marino. And I'm five feet nine and a half." She almost added, as she had as a teenager, "Wanna make something out of it?" But the look in his eye made her curb her tongue. Too, she was momentarily fascinated with the way the mist glittered on the surface of his hair like diamond chips on black velvet.

The corner of his eyes crinkled. "You're just a little squirt. My mama has you beat by half an inch." He picked up the suitcases she'd dropped. "Why don't you unlock the door, and I'll unload your things."

She grabbed a duffel bag from the heap in the wagon and hurried around to the front of the cabin. She pushed the door open and turned on a light, expecting the worst. She was pleasantly surprised to find that the large room was simple but amazingly clean and homey. A patchwork quilt covered the double bed set against one wall with an oak nightstand and dresser. In one corner a small sofa and an easy chair were grouped with a coffee table on a braided rug. In the space carved out next to the bathroom at the back there was a small kitchenette and a sturdy table with four chairs.

"Where do you want this?" Shade asked, hefting a large box into the room.

"Careful, that's my computer. Just set it down anywhere. I'll unpack it later."

"What do you use a computer for?"

She hesitated, wondering how much of the truth to tell him. Part of it, she decided. After all, what connection could someone from the backwoods of East Texas have with anyone in New York? "I'm a writer."

He frowned. "What kind of writer?"

Catching the faint sharpness and suspicion tingeing his question, she backed off. "I . . . I'm writing a novel. A mystery."

His features relaxed. "Sounds interesting. Do you have anything published?"

"This is my first book," she answered, hedging.

He smiled. "I'll look forward to buying a copy."

She felt like a dirty dog for lying to him.

Working together, they soon had the station wagon emptied of all her belongings, including the precious boxes of files, notes, and tapes that were worth her life—literally.

Byline howled inside his carrier. She ignored him and reached for her purse. Pulling out a five-dollar bill, she offered it to Shade with her thanks for his assistance.

Looking amused, he shook his head. "Glad to help a neighbor."

"You don't work here?"

"Nope. I'm in cabin one."

"Oh. Are you on vacation?"

He shrugged. "I suppose you might say that."

Byline yowled louder. Maggie opened the door to the cage, and the cat shot out like a furry bullet and lodged himself under the bed.

"You stupid cat!" She got on her hands and knees and tried to coax him out. He hissed and bit her finger. She yelped and banged her head on the bed frame. "Ungrateful wretch!"

She scooted backward and sat on the floor, resting her forehead against her knees. She rubbed her crown with both hands feeling a bump rising amid the mass of damp corkscrew curls.

"Are you hurt?" Shade asked, kneeling beside her.

She jumped up and turned away. "I'm fine." But she wasn't fine. She was miserable. She was broke, filthy, scared—though she'd rather be boiled in oil than admit it to anyone—and hundreds of miles away from everything that was familiar.

"You don't look fine," he said softly, and gently turned her to face him. "You look like you could use a hug."

She automatically stiffened and pulled back. She knew nothing about this man.

"Just a hug," he said. "A friendly hug. No more. Everybody needs a hug now and then."

He pulled her against him and wrapped his arms around her. The rock-solid strength of him swaddled her in a wondrous warm cocoon of security. She reveled in the feeling. Everything in her experience screamed for her to pull back, to end this abruptly and toss him out on his ear. But some starving part of her urged her to hold on to him, to hug him back. Instinctively she knew that she could trust this man. He was like a huge tree rooted firmly in the earth, offering his shelter.

For long moments, she simply stood there encased in the comforting power that emanated from him. From somewhere deep inside her a trickle of emotion began to emerge. It flowed through her, swelling, gathering momentum until it grew into a raging river, overwhelming her, bursting through old barriers with a loud sob.

She clung to this stranger who offered her comfort, and for the first time in twenty years, Maggie Marino wept.

TWO

Shade's throat tightened and his chest ached as he held the sobbing woman in his arms. From the little he knew of her, he suspected that she wasn't the type who cried easily. He could feel the bone-deep despair that wrenched the tears from her, and his gut knotted.

A part of him, the part that he thought had been recivilized years ago, wanted to lash out and destroy whatever made her cry. Instead, he laid his cheek against damp hair that was drying to the deep rust of an old penny and rubbed her back. "Shhh, darlin', everything is going to be okay. Nothing can be that bad."

As if his words had broken a spell, she stiffened in his arms and pushed him away. "Easy for you to say. And don't call me darling. I don't appreciate the familiarity, and I'm not a child to be coddled."

Not replying to the defensive bite of her words, he watched her struggle for control. Her fingers curled into tight fists, and she sucked in a shuddering breath. He lifted her chin and said, "I've got a good ear if you want to talk about it."

A combative spark flashed in her eyes, changing them to the color of fine fiery bourbon and drying her tears. She jerked from his grasp. "There's nothing to talk about. I'm simply exhausted. I'm not in the habit of weeping in a stranger's arms. Now, if you'll excuse me, I'd like to take a shower."

He smiled at her bravado. "I'm not a stranger. We're neighbors. Around here, neighbors help each other."

She pursed her lips and glared at him. "Well, where I come from, they mind their own business. Thank you for helping me move my things in, and close the door on your way out."

He lifted an eyebrow. "All full of piss and vinegar again, are we?" He strolled to the door. "Supper will be ready when you are."

Outside, Shade shook his head and chuckled. He had a hunch that the next few weeks would be interesting with Ms. Maggie Marino around. Even sopping wet and with mud on her cheek, she was an attractive lady. He liked the strong chin that jutted at the least provocation, the flashing eyes that tilted up at the corners, the faint sprinkle of copper freckles that dusted an upturned nose, softening her strong features. But more than her looks, something about her he couldn't quite put a name to stimulated his interest more than any woman he'd met in years.

When Shade walked into the kitchen, Buck was dredging pounded hunks of round steak in flour and tossing them into a skillet of hot grease.

Buck looked up from his task and said, "Want to explain now why I needed to hire a cook? I know I ain't much of a hand at it, but you do a pretty fair job when it's your turn."

Shade leaned against the counter. "I don't know, Sarge. Something in her eyes got to me."

"Her *eyes*?" Buck snorted. "I figure it was what was in that wet shirt that got to you."

"Wet shirt? I didn't notice."

Buck snorted again. "Like hell you didn't. You'd have to be blind or dead not to notice. Cleaned up and dried out, she'll be a fine-looking woman."

"But she's got a tongue sharper than bear grass." Shade started gathering dishes to set the table. "My gut tells me she's carrying around a bushel of misery. I have a hunch that she's running away from something."

"Like you are?"

Shade shrugged. "Maybe. And I'd just as soon

she didn't know who I am, so don't mention my name."

"Wild horses wouldn't drag it out of me. I know you're in-cog-nita."

Shade laughed affectionately at the ex-Marine who had been like a favorite uncle to him since he was eighteen. "Maybe I'm getting soft in my old age, but I want to help her. I'll pay for her keep."

"Naw," Buck said, forking the meat and turning it in the smoking grease. "I owe old Silas to help out his niece, and if it wasn't for you shelling out the cash, I wouldn't even have this place."

"But if you hadn't saved my ass in 'Nam, I'd be playing poker with Saint Peter and you wouldn't be walking with a limp."

"As I recall, you saved my bacon a couple of times too," Buck said gruffly. "Hand me that platter and get outta my way. I've got to make gravy. Or do you want to make it?"

Shade grinned. "I'll let you do the honors. The lumps will convince Ms. Marino that we really do need a cook."

They really did need a cook, Maggie thought as she sawed on a blackened piece of meat that could have been used for a roofing tile. The gravy had the taste and consistency of lumpy wallpaper paste and did little to disguise the scorched potatoes. The green beans—at least she assumed they were green beans—had been boiled to a limp moss-colored heap and were swimming in bacon fat. If she hadn't been starving, she would have dumped the whole mess in the garbage. As it was, she managed to eat enough to take the edge off her hunger.

"How about a piece of apple pie?" Buck asked when the meal was finished.

Shade winked at Maggie. "It's one Sybil baked and left in the freezer before she went to Shreveport."

She brightened. "I'd love a piece of pie."

In fact, she ate two pieces. It was heavenly.

When she'd scraped the last crumb from her plate, Maggie glanced up to see Shade grinning over his coffee mug. Dear Lord, she wished he wouldn't smile like that; it did funny things to her insides.

"What's so amusing?" she asked sharply.

His grin widened. "I surely do like to see a woman enjoy her food."

"The pie was quite delicious." She turned to Buck. "I'd love to have your wife's recipe."

Buck scratched his head. "I don't rightly think Sybil has a recipe. She just puts things together. I gotta get cleaned up here before the regular

Tuesday night domino bunch comes in." He rose, picked up his plate, and headed around the bar to the kitchen.

"I'll help," Maggie said, following him. "I need to check the supplies so I can plan the rest of the week's menus and make a grocery list. What sorts of things do you like?"

"Oh, I'll eat pert near anything. Except tripe, brains, and mountain oysters. Don't care much for them."

Maggie shuddered at the thought of eating brains, and she had a vague idea that tripe was also something ghastly, but she'd never heard of mountain oysters. "What are mountain oysters?"

Buck looked sheepish, and behind her, Shade laughed. "Don't ask."

"Why not? It sounds like a contradiction in terms. I thought all oysters came from oceans and bays. I've never heard of oysters from the mountains."

Shade cleared his throat. "Mountain oysters are bull testicles. Some people like them fried."

Maggie rolled her eyes and groaned. "God will strike me dead before I'd cook or eat anything so gross." She glanced around. "Where's the garbage disposal?"

"Over yonder." He motioned with his head toward the sad-eyed hound who stood wagging his tail and drooling.

Buck scraped the scraps of their meal into a large bowl, added dried dog food, and set the dish on the porch outside the kitchen.

"Handy," Maggie said, watching the process. "I hope there's a dishwasher." She looked around, seeing none.

Shade pointed to a deep sink and picked up a bottle of green detergent. "The old-fashioned kind. We've been taking turns. When Buck cooks, I clean, and vice versa. I'm glad that he hired you; I was getting dishpan hands."

Maggie looked heavenward and thought, *I went to Columbia School of Journalism for this?* Rubber gloves went at the top of her grocery list.

An hour later, the dishes clean and her supply check completed, Maggie dug through a box of books in her cabin. Byline rubbed against her, then sat looking at her with his I-need-to-get-out-and-go-exploring look. "A bear might eat you out there," she told him.

Byline didn't seem to believe her. He trotted to the front door and waited.

"Oh, all right, you stubborn cat. But if you get lost, don't blame me." She opened the door, and he zipped through it and out into the dark. Byline was as independent and recalcitrant as she, and maybe, she thought, that was why they got along so well. But those very characteristics had cost her job.

She went back to digging through another of the boxes. Thankfully, she found what she was looking for: Two cookbooks in almost pristine condition and a file of yellowed clippings from her stint as food editor years ago. She heaved a sigh of relief.

The truth was, Maggie wasn't much of a cook. The inside of her oven at home was dusty, and she'd never even had to clean the drip pans under the burners. Most of the time she ate out, grabbed something from the corner deli, or nuked a frozen dinner in the microwave.

Oh, if pushed, she could do something simple like broil a steak or a chop and toss a salad, but she rarely had since she and John had divorced several years before. Even then, either John, who fancied himself as a gourmet, or the housekeeper did most of the meal preparation. To placate her ex-husband, she had learned to prepare one "company meal," but God forbid that the same people showed up a second time.

Maggie had always had more important things to occupy her time than sweating over pots—which was one of the myriad reasons that she and John had decided that she'd never be the proper corporate wife he wanted. She didn't enjoy sipping cocktails at high society charity events. She didn't work out at luxurious health clubs; she got her exercise chasing stories or playing basketball with the troubled kids at Tree Hollow.

She fixed herself a cup of instant coffee, set the cookbooks and file on the table, and went to work poring over the pages. Soup and sandwiches for lunch. Oh, great, there was a whole section in one of the books on luncheon soups and sandwiches. She found several interesting ones that seemed easy, and made notations.

Something more complicated for dinner. Tomorrow night, she'd fix her "company meal." She was fairly comfortable with that one. She ferreted out a few other dishes that appeared simple. What could be so difficult about cooking? Any idiot with half a brain could read a recipe and follow directions.

It was well after midnight before she completed her menus and had made a grocery list. Exhausted, she stripped off her clothes, leaving them in heaps on her way to bed.

With the quilt pulled up to her chin, she allowed her body to relax. She discovered that, even here in a strange place and a strange bed, for the first time in weeks, she felt safe and secure.

What had started out two and a half months before as an investigative foray into the goings-on at Tree Hollow, a charitable institute for runaways and troubled teens, had turned out to be a nightmare. Because she had a soft spot in her heart for the place that had turned her life around when she was a kid, Maggie had donated time and money to the Hollow for the last several years. And the kids trusted her, confided in her. As she began piecing together the stories they told her and digging into the facts, she knew that the makings of a major scandal brewed behind the walls of the respected organization—drugs, sexual exploitation. There might be a case, too, that the institute was being used for money laundering—and that could lead to a mob connection or a drug cartel. With her editor's blessing, she started to work. She discovered that some *very* prestigious names among the New York elite were involved, including the publisher of her own newspaper.

When that little gem turned up, her editor, after several high-level, closed-door meetings, had told her to back off the story. She'd refused and had been fired on the spot. When she'd continued digging, she'd begun to receive sinister phone calls. When that didn't work, the threats grew more serious. And frightening. But she was safe now. Nobody would think to look for Maggie Marino in a place like this. Not in a million years.

The last images that floated through her mind were of a smiling face with a dark mustache and soft green eyes and of a pair of strong arms around her.

Rattling noises from the cabin door jerked Maggie awake. Her heart pounding, she sat straight up in bed as the door swung open. She was ready to scream bloody murder when a young woman with short blond curls and a pug nose stepped inside.

"Ooops, sorry," the young woman said. "I came to clean your room. I thought you'd be up by now."

Maggie plopped back down on the pillow. "Come back when it's a decent hour. Like noon."

The girl, who looked no more than eighteen, giggled. "I can't do that. I have to be at the college for my history class by nine, and it's almost eight now. Why don't I just clean around you? I'll be quiet as a mouse."

Mumbling her assent, Maggie flopped over on her stomach. She tried to go back to sleep, but she was wide awake. The girl's off-key humming as she cleaned the bathroom did nothing to help. Giving up, Maggie rose and pulled on a pair of jeans and a blue cotton sweater, then stuck her hot coil in a cup of water in the kitchenette.

The girl came out of the bathroom, and her

eyes widened when she saw Maggie. "Oh, I hope I didn't disturb you too much."

"No problem. I'm a night person, and I don't function well in the mornings, at least until I've had a cup of coffee."

"I'm Omie Nell Slack. I work here mornings before class and on weekends. Shade told me you were going to be working here too. Isn't he just the cutest thing you've ever seen?"

Maggie thought of the dark-haired man, and a little shiver prickled her neck. Cute wasn't a word she'd use to describe him, but it seemed as though she wasn't the only one who found Shade attractive. She stuck out her hand. "I'm Maggie Marino, the new cook."

Omie Nell giggled as they shook hands. "You don't look much like a cook."

"With apologies to Gloria Steinem for corrupting her quote: This is what a cook looks like." Maggie posed with her arms outstretched.

Omie Nell giggled again and went about her chores while Maggie fixed her coffee and tried to do something with her curly mop of hair. She finally gave up and tied it back with a scarf. Trying to sound casual, she asked, "Is Shade going to be here long on his vacation?"

"Vacation? Well, I wouldn't know about that. He never said."

"How long has he been here?"

Omie Nell leaned on her dust mop. "I'm not sure of that either. He was here when I started to work four months ago." She rolled her eyes. "All the ladies in these parts think he's *heavenly*. Sooo sexy. And those eyes. Don't they just go right through you?"

Disgusted with herself for bringing up his name and having to listen to the girl gush, Maggie mumbled something and escaped to the bathroom.

A few minutes later, she peeked out and was relieved to find her room empty. She gathered up her purse and the grocery list.

As she stepped out the door, a deep voice said, "Good morning."

She glanced toward the porch of the next cabin, which was only a few yards away. Shade sat with his feet propped on the rail, his chair leaned back on two legs. Byline was draped across his lap, purring so loudly from Shade's stroking that Maggie could hear him from where she stood.

"Good morning," she replied. "I hope the cat's not bothering you."

"Not at all." He grinned. "But I'm not so sure that Comet is too fond of him."

"Comet?"

"My hound."

"That's an odd name for a dog that has to think for half a day before he moves."

Shade laughed. "Oh, he can move when the time is right. He just conserves his energy. There were eight in his litter. Dancer and Prancer—"

"And Comet and Cupid. I get it." She walked over to where the two of them were lounging. "I'll put him in my cabin." She started to pick up Byline, then hesitated. Unless she grabbed the cat's head or tail, scooping him from the delicate position in Shade's lap would be . . . awkward.

He seemed to grasp her dilemma, but the wretch did nothing to help. He only grinned.

"Get down, Byline," she commanded.

The cat opened one eye briefly, then closed it. He didn't stir.

Damned stupid cat, she thought. "Byline, down!" She might as well have spoken to the Statue of Liberty.

Shade chuckled, but he didn't move either. "Cats are ornery, independent creatures, aren't they? Now you take a dog, a dog will mind. Need some help?"

Irritation shot through her. She'd like to tell this . . . rube exactly what she thought of his offer, but she wouldn't give him the satisfaction. "Certainly not," she said sweetly.

She scooped up the cat, jamming her right hand between jean bulge and fur with considerably more force than was necessary. He winced; she smirked.

"Don't try your cutesy games with me, buster. I didn't arrive this morning on a banana boat."

Feigning an innocent, surprised look, he said, "Games? What games? I don't know what you're talking about."

"Like hell you don't!" She stomped off with the cat. "Troublemaker," she muttered to Byline as she deposited him in her cabin. "Your breakfast is in the kitchen."

She'd have rather had her fingernails pulled out than to admit that an impression of rough denim and well-endowed man clung to the back of her hand, or that her heart seemed to have increased in tempo. Oh, Shade might be momentarily titillating with his rugged brand of sex appeal, but he wasn't her type. She preferred men who could speak in words of more than two syllables. In any case, with everything else on her mind, she wasn't about to give him any encouragement.

Ignoring Shade who still sat on his porch, strumming on a guitar now, she got into the station wagon and turned the key.

Nothing happened.

She tried again.

Nothing. Not even a cough or a sputter.

Maggie banged her hand against the steering wheel. "Damned piece of junk!"

She pumped the gas pedal and tried again. Still nothing. She got out and slammed the door, spouting colorful phrases about the wagon's parentage.

Shade stood at the entrance to the carport. "Problems?"

"The car won't start."

"Want me to take a look at it?" he asked.

She detested having to ask for help, especially from him. "I need to get to the grocery store right away if I'm going to be back in time to fix lunch."

"Come on." He gestured sideways with his head. "I'll take you. It's a little too far to walk."

She hesitated.

He chuckled. "We'll take a chaperon." He let out an ear-splitting whistle, and Comet came bounding from the woods like his namesake.

They drove to town in Shade's big silver pickup, Comet sitting on the front seat between them with his tongue hanging out, looking happy as a clam.

The twelve-mile drive to the supermarket in the nearest town was quiet except for the country music wailing from the radio and Comet's excited panting.

When they pulled into the parking lot, Maggie said, "I forgot to ask Buck if he has any Grand Marnier in the bar. Do you know if he does?"

Shade gave a bark of laughter. "I doubt it. Buck's clientele doesn't go in much for liqueurs. Want me to pick up some while you get the groceries?"

"I would appreciate it."

"No problem. The liquor store is right next to the tackle shop, and I need to get a couple of things. I'll meet you at the checkout line."

Shopping took longer than she anticipated, but at least she was able to find everything on her list—except watercress, fresh basil, and a couple of other items. She could improvise.

By the time they arrived home with the groceries, it was after eleven o'clock, and she would have to hurry to have lunch prepared by twelve.

"Need some help?" Shade asked as he brought in the last sack.

"No, thank you. I prefer solitude when I cook."

Shade shrugged. "Fine with me. Buck's in the bait shop, and I'll be shooting pool. Give a holler if you need anything."

Don't hold your breath, she thought. She could handle this. Piece of cake.

It took her a couple of minutes to figure out how the huge butane stove worked, then she put six eggs to boiling on a back burner while she stashed the things she'd bought. She didn't know exactly how long it would take a chicken to cook for broth, so she decided to use canned stock instead. She washed and sliced fresh mushrooms, and set them aside. So far, so good.

She couldn't precisely remember how much onion, celery, carrots went next, so she decided to run to her room for the cookbooks. At the same time she could take along the milk and cereal she'd bought for herself. And Byline's cat food.

She found Comet barking and pawing at the window of her cabin. Byline was sitting on the windowsill inside, swishing his tail and taunting the dog.

"Quiet, Comet!" Maggie commanded.

The dog stopped barking, but he didn't look happy about it. Byline seemed to grin down at the dog and rubbed his head against the glass. Comet growled.

When Maggie opened the door, Comet scrambled through the opening, knocking her down. The paper sack broke, cans of cat food rolled every which way and pandemonium broke loose as Comet chased Byline around the room. Maggie yelled and lunged for the dog, missed, and went sprawling.

Byline sped to the kitchenette and bounded from table to counter to refrigerator top. Comet, after discovering that he couldn't reach his quarry, barked, then started baying to raise the dead.

"What in the hell is going on in here?" Shade asked as he came running in.

Maggie pushed herself up from the floor and glared at him. "Your damned dog is trying to kill my cat and maim me. Get him out of here!"

Shade spoke sharply to Comet, then grabbed him by the collar and dragged him to the door. "Are you okay?" he asked Maggie.

"I'm fine. Just go away." She started picking up items from the broken sack.

"I'm sorry about that. They don't seem to get along very well."

Maggie only gave him an exasperated look and shooed man and dog out the door. She quickly stowed the milk in the refrigerator, glaring up at Byline. "You're not an innocent party in this."

Grabbing the cookbooks, she rushed back to the kitchen, knowing that if she didn't hurry, lunch was going to be very late.

She found an iron skillet and tossed a half stick of margarine in to melt while she searched for a food processor. There was none. Instead she began hand chopping onions, celery, carrots, and garlic. She was dicing celery when she smelled something funny.

The margarine!

She ran to the stove where black smoke billowed from the pan. Grabbing the skillet, she seared her fingers and dropped the heavy pan in the middle of the floor, cursing and shaking her hand.

Suddenly, a loud explosion like a shotgun blast ripped through the room.

Dear God, they'd found her! She hit the floor and covered her head.

"Holy hell! What's happening in here? World War Three?" Shade yelled as he came running in.

"They're shooting at me! Get down!"

THREE

Shade started laughing. "Who's winning the battle, you or the eggs?"

Maggie uncovered her head and looked up just as a blob fell from the ceiling and hit her nose.

"The eggs! I forgot about the eggs. What happened?"

"Looks like they boiled dry and exploded. I turned the burner off. You have three left. How many did you start with?"

"Six."

He offered his hand to help her up. She winced when he touched her fingers. "What's wrong?"

"I burned myself. Nothing major."

He looked at her hand, then led her to the sink and broke off a piece of a potted plant on the windowsill. "This is aloe vera," he told her as he split open the fleshy spine and slowly rubbed the sap over her fingers. "Sybil keeps it here for burns."

When he held her hand to his mouth and blew on it, the sting from her fingers disappeared, but another one nettled her scalp and a rash of goose bumps broke out all over her body. She became overwhelmingly aware of his nearness, the warmth generated by his large body, the smell of him.

She glanced from her hand to his eyes. They were the soft green of ocean spray, enticing, fathomless. And watching her. His gaze still locked with hers, he blew again. The coolness of his breath and the blatantly provocative gesture sent a ripple up her spine.

His eyes, heavy lidded and growing darker in their centers, held hers as he brought her fingers to his lips and softly kissed each one. Her breath caught.

"My mama always said that kissing hurts made them better," he said in a rusty murmur that made the cliché sound like love words.

Maggie felt herself melting and almost sighed aloud.

"'Bout time to eat?" Buck asked from behind them.

She jerked her hand away and jumped back. "I'm running a bit late. I'll have things together in a few minutes."

Buck picked up the heavy iron skillet. "What's Sybil's corn bread pan doing on the floor?"

"Corn bread pan?" Maggie asked.

"Yep. She keeps it seasoned up just right and don't allow nobody to cook nothin' in it but corn bread—to keep it from sticking, you know."

"It looks like I goofed. I was going to sauté some vegetables in it, but I burned my hand before I could."

"No harm done," Shade said. "Frying pans are down here." He opened a lower cabinet. "Want some help?"

"No thanks, I have everything under control." Like hell she did, she thought, but what Maggie Marino started, she finished. "You guys run along. I'll call you when things are ready."

Buck glanced around at the damage from the exploding eggs and looked skeptical; Shade hesitated. She gestured them from the room and went back to her chopping. She'd never realized that dicing vegetables took so long. Canned soup had always been good enough for her.

It was almost one-thirty before she blew a strand of hair from her eyes and sprinkled Parmesan cheese on the lemon slice floating atop the soup. The stuff looked a little watery, but she'd followed the recipe exactly.

She hoped it was edible because there would be plenty left over for lunch the next day. And the next.

Around each bowl, she arranged the egg salad on toast points from which she'd trimmed the crusts and scraped the burned spots. Remembering that John had said about a million times that presentation was everything, she added a couple of sprigs of parsley and a cherry tomato. And the plates did look rather attractive, she thought, as she carried one for each of the hungry men who sat waiting at a table in the bar.

Buck frowned as he looked down at the meal, then cleared his throat. "Right pretty. Uh . . ." He cleared his throat again. "What is it?"

Shade made a funny, coughing sound.

"Lemon-basil mushroom soup and egg salad with apples and walnuts."

"I don't allow as how I've ever had that," Buck said. "Mighty interesting. Where's the ice tea?"

"Iced tea?"

"Always like ice tea with my meals."

Shade made the sound again. "Why don't you have water, Buck? I think all that caffeine is what's been keeping you awake nights."

"Huh? Oh, yeah. I'll bet you're right. Water would hit the spot." He gave Maggie a big grin.

"Coming right up," she said.

When everyone was served, Maggie picked up her spoon and waited while the men tasted the soup.

Buck raised his eyebrows. "You know this stuff ain't half bad."

"Very tasty," Shade added.

Maggie beamed. "There's plenty for seconds."

About three o'clock Shade walked through the door that led from the tavern to the bait shop. Buck was munching peanut butter and crackers. An empty Vienna sausage can sat on the counter by his elbow.

Shade laughed. "Hungry already?"

Buck rubbed his belly. "I guess I ain't used to eatin' Yankee food. It sure don't stick to your ribs much, does it?"

Maggie barely had cleaned up the mess from lunch when she had to start preparations for dinner. Buck had said he liked to eat at six, and she was determined to have the meal ready on the dot. She put asparagus tips and sliced water chestnuts in the fridge to chill, then washed and dried romaine leaves, prepared sweet red peppers, and stowed them in the crisper. With a bottled dressing, that would take care of the salad.

Iced tea. She wouldn't forget iced tea, though she usually served her company meal with a nice Chablis. And candlelight. She thought for a moment. No. That was too much. Somehow she couldn't see Buck and Shade eating in the tavern by candlelight.

While she was peeling carrots, Shade ambled in, wiping his hands on a greasy rag. "I got your wagon started," he said. "Battery cables were corroded."

She wrinkled her nose. "Sounds gruesome. Is it serious?"

He snitched a carrot from her growing pile. "Not too serious if that were the only problem. I tinkered with it some, but your car needs a major overhaul."

"But I've only had the darned thing a week and a half."

"Somebody saw you coming. You got a lemon."

She snorted. "Don't I know it."

He leaned against the counter near where she worked and crunched on his carrot. She tried to keep her eyes on her task, but they seemed to veer his way of their own accord. There was definitely something magnetic about him.

Maybe it was the elaborate cobra tattoo coiled

around his upper arm that fascinated her. Intertwined with a purple flower, it seemed quietly dangerous and a little wicked. Like him, she thought.

"Where did you get the tattoo?" she asked.

He glanced down at it as if he'd forgotten that it was there. "Saigon."

The terseness of his answer indicated that he'd prefer to drop the topic, but inquisitiveness was too deeply ingrained in Maggie to let it slide. "You were in Vietnam?"

"Yep."

"Army?"

"Marines."

"How long were you there?"

"Too long."

"You must have been very young," she said.

He shrugged, and she sensed that the subject was closed. She tried to focus her attention on the carrots, but when he stretched and rubbed his hand across his chest, her gaze followed his fingers as they slid over the fabric of the faded red jersey with the sleeves ripped out. Beneath the grease streaks, she could make out a very dim HARVARD ROWING TEAM emblazoned across his shirt. She almost laughed aloud. His muscled arms looked as if he would have been a fine oarsman, but she suspected that he'd picked up the shirt at a thrift store.

"Know where Harvard is?" she dared to ask him.

"Well, Miss Maggie, as I recollect, it's somewhere up in Yankeeland close to Boston." He grinned and reached for another carrot.

She swatted his hand away. "Score one for you. And please don't call me Miss Maggie. It sounds like something from *Gone with the Wind.* My name is Maggie. Just plain Maggie. And speaking of names, I don't even know yours. I've only heard you called Shade, which I presume is a nickname. What *is* your name?"

"Shade is good enough."

His evasion piqued her natural curiosity. "But your mother must have called you something else. Everybody has at least a first name and a last."

"Ah, Just Plain Maggie, don't fret yourself about it." He tapped her nose. "What's in a name? That which we call a rose, by any other name would smell as sweet." He swiped another carrot and ambled from the room.

With his brows drawn together, Buck stared at his plate. "Exactly what is that thing?"

"It's an artichoke," Shade told him. "You eat it like this." Shade pulled off a leaf and demonstrated.

Maggie watched as Buck tried it. "Not bad,

but it seems like an awful lot of trouble for no more than that." He glanced up at Maggie. "The carrots are real appetizing. Pretty, too, but they've got a kick to them."

Maggie laughed, relieved that he appreciated her Grand Marnier and orange marmalade sauce. But when he picked up a lamb chop and devoured it in two bites, then demolished the other one just as quickly, she grew alarmed.

"I believe them's the littlest pork chops I've ever seen. Got any more?"

Shade gave a strangled cough and kept his eyes on his plate.

Maggie said, "Why don't you take mine. I'm not very hungry." She quickly transferred her meat to Buck's plate.

Buck looked stricken. "Oh, no, Miss Maggie. I've had plenty. Sybil is always telling me I make a pig of myself." He patted his big belly. "Wouldn't hurt me to lose a few pounds."

Maggie insisted, and they finished their meal in awkward silence. She reminded herself to double portions from then on. She wasn't used to such hearty eaters. Everybody she knew was always on a diet. Thank heavens she'd decided to serve one of Sybil's cobblers she'd found in the freezer rather than make the poached pears she usually had for dessert. They ate every bite of it.

When Shade strolled into the kitchen later,

she was absently washing a plate and staring out the window, wondering how she'd ever gotten into such a mess. He picked up a towel and started drying the dishes in the drainer.

"You look about a million miles away," he said.

"No, only several hundred. Dinner didn't go any better than lunch, did it?"

"Dinner was excellent. It's just that Buck is used to simple country fare and plenty of it. He doesn't have a sophisticated palate," he said gently.

She glanced at the tall man standing beside her at the sink, trying to figure him out. "But *you* do?"

He shrugged. "I've been around more than he has. He's more comfortable with roast beef and hot dogs than with lamb chops and egg salad with apples and walnuts."

She brightened. "Hot dogs? I'm a whiz with hot dogs."

He laughed and picked up another dish. "There you go."

But at lunch the following day, Buck stared at the sauerkraut on his four hot dogs and asked, "Where's the chili?"

This wasn't working out.

After the disastrous lunch, Maggie was determined to fix something that Buck wouldn't gawk at—and she had the distinct feeling he would turn up his nose at the stir-fry with cashews that she'd planned. Roast beef, Shade had said. She scrounged through the big freezer and found a large package wrapped in white paper and labeled "Chuck Roast." That should do it. And potatoes. Any fool could bake a potato.

She wasn't sure how long to cook the beef, but about an hour per pound sounded good. How much did the darned thing weigh?

Hefting a five-pound package of sugar in one hand and the roast in the other, she estimated they were about the same. She located a roasting pan and placed the frozen slab of meat on the rack. Three hundred and fifty degrees seemed to ring a bell as an appropriate temperature, but she decided to turn the oven to four hundred and fifty to compensate for its being frozen.

There, she thought, feeling inordinately proud of herself. She would bake the potatoes in the last hour, and while they were cooking, she would steam broccoli and make a cheese sauce. They could have ice cream for dessert.

Satisfied that she had this cooking business down to a fine art, Maggie went to her cabin to finish unpacking her books and research material and set up her computer.

She worked until her alarm went off at a quarter to five, then went back to the kitchen. The roast smelled nice. After placing baking potatoes on the top rack and preparing broccoli for last-minute steaming, she decided to check the meat for doneness. She lifted the uncovered roaster from the oven to the counter.

The meat looked kind of strange. Curled and brown. And considerably smaller. She stuck a big fork in the middle and tried to cut it. Damn!

She threw the knife down and it went skidding across the floor as she uttered a few well-chosen curses.

Pool cue in hand, Shade leaned against the doorjamb and asked, "Problems?"

Maggie glared at him, then held up the roast with a big fork. "Do you happen to know if Roy Rogers needs a new saddle?"

Shade threw back his head and laughed.

"I don't see what's so damned funny! That's supposed to be our dinner."

He found a large pot and ran water into it. "Chop up a couple of onions."

"What are you going to do?"

He winked at her. "My mama always said that if life handed you a lemon, make lemonade."

Buck took a bite, then broke into a big smile. "Miss Maggie, I believe that's the best golldurned hash I ever ate. As good as Sybil's. Better maybe."

Maggie glanced at Shade. He only winked and said, "It's very good."

"But what am I going to do for an encore?" she mumbled.

"I'm right partial to chicken and dumplings," Buck said, hinting broadly.

"Chicken and dumplings?" Maggie pasted a bright smile on her face. "No problem." She glanced at Shade, but he only grinned and winked again.

If she hadn't been so hungry, she'd have hit him over the head with her plate. She hadn't the foggiest notion how to make chicken and dumplings nor did she remember seeing a recipe in her cookbooks.

"With cookin' this good," Buck said between shoveling in bites of food, "I'm surprised a pretty gal like you ain't married." He looked at Shade, then glanced at Maggie. "You ain't married, are ya?"

"No."

"Ever been?"

"Once. It didn't work out."

"Any kids?"

"No." Maggie squirmed, uncomfortable with the inquisition.

"Ain't that a co-in-ci-dence. Shade here was

married once too. His didn't work out neither. Shame. I wouldn't take the world for my wife and kids. Why, I think—"

"Buck," Shade interrupted, "did you know that Maggie is a writer? She's writing a mystery novel."

"You don't say. That's right inter-resting. Is that what you did in New York City? Write mystery stories?"

"Oh, I did a little of this and a little of that. You know how it is with writers. Tell me, Buck, are you from this area originally?"

"This river bottom is my stompin' grounds. Born and raised about five miles from here. Sybil too. She was my high school sweetheart."

"So you've lived here all your life?"

"'Cept for the seventeen-year hitch I served in the Marines. That was near 'bout twenty years ago. Been right here ever since."

"And you, Shade," she said, turning her attention to the man on her right, "are these your stomping grounds as well?"

"Occasionally."

"Then you weren't born and reared here?" she asked.

"Nope."

"Shade?" Buck cackled. "He's a ci—"

"Didn't I hear you say we were having ice cream for dessert?" Shade asked.

Maggie glanced from Buck, who looked sheepish, to Shade, who sat expressionless. Curious. Very curious. "Vanilla with chocolate sauce. Have you two known each other for a long time?"

"Yep." Shade scraped his chair back and picked up his plate. "I'll help you with the ice cream."

She kept her seat. "Did you meet when you were in the Marines?"

Buck grabbed his plate and charged for the kitchen.

Shade chuckled. "You surely are a nosy little thing. You know what they say about curiosity, don't you?"

She gave him a haughty look. "By no stretch of the imagination am I a 'little thing.' And I'm well aware of that old saw about curiosity and cats, but I prefer to think, like Johnson, that curiosity is a characteristic of a vigorous intellect."

"Johnson? Lyndon or Arte?" He grinned.

"Samuel."

Shade's eyes shone with a mischievous twinkle. "Old Sam was before my time. How about some ice cream?"

She didn't budge. "Did you and Buck meet in the Marines?"

"Yep."

She stood and grabbed her plate. "There,

that wasn't so painful, was it?" She strode toward the kitchen.

As she dug ice cream from the carton, Maggie wondered why Shade was so blasted secretive. It had been her experience that people as closemouthed as he was usually had something to hide. Her questions about his past had been perfectly innocuous, yet he always managed to sidestep them. She hadn't missed how he interrupted the more gregarious Buck either. If he'd known her, Shade would have been more forthcoming, because enigmas only piqued her interest and made her determined to ferret out the story. Why didn't he want her to know his name or anything about his past? Exactly what was Shade hiding?

As they were finishing dessert, two customers came in for a beer. While Buck played bartender, Maggie and Shade cleared the table and carried the dishes to the kitchen. They fell into an easy routine with her washing and him drying.

"I appreciate the help with dinner," Maggie said. "I was sure that it was a lost cause." She smiled at him. "How are you with chicken and dumplings?"

"Fair. My mother probably makes the world's best."

"Oh?" Trying to act blasé, she asked, "Which recipe does she use?"

"My grandmother's."

"Oh."

They washed and dried in silence for a few minutes, then Maggie tried another approach. "Did your mother teach you to cook?"

"Yep."

"Isn't that unusual?"

He shrugged.

"I thought that around here sons learned to shoot and fish and spit, and daughters learned to cook and sew and wash."

He chuckled. "Around here?"

"Texas, I mean."

"I hope you don't let the governor hear you say that. I don't know about the spitting, but she's a darned good shot. And my mother, like a lot of Texas women, was egalitarian long before it was popular."

Egalitarian? Maggie's eyebrows went up at his use of the word.

"Mama insisted that her boys learn how to cook and wash and sew well enough to replace a button. We even had to iron our own shirts."

"I'm lousy at ironing."

Shade gave her a lopsided grin. "Can you spit?"

She laughed. "Better than I can sew." Or cook, she added mentally. "You have brothers?"

"Yep. Two."

"Sisters?"

"Nope. What about you?"

She shook her head. "I occasionally had foster brothers and sisters, but they never lasted long. My father never had been around, and after my mother died, I was in several foster homes until I was fifteen."

"What happened when you were fifteen?"

"I ran away from a deplorable situation. I lived on the streets for a year, taking odd jobs when I could. Things were pretty bad until I found Tree Hollow."

"Tree Hollow?"

"Mmm." It was Maggie's turn to be silent.

"Sounds like a refuge for a rabbit."

She laughed. "That's not too far off the mark. It is . . . was a wonderful place for runaways and troubled kids. They helped me get my life together and finish my education." She handed him the last pot and stripped off her rubber gloves.

"Sounds like a fine organization."

"It was." *Was* being the operative word, she thought. The travesty of the current Tree Hollow made her angry as hell. Furious. Despite all the warnings, she was going to expose the sleazy operations rampant in the institution. She clenched her teeth in renewed determination.

"You look as tense as a June bug in a chicken coop. Want to go for a walk with me?"

"Walk?" she asked, lost in her thoughts.

"It's a nice evening. A walk along the river always has a soothing effect on me. Want to give it a try?"

He was smiling that smile again, the one that made her insides flip. Why did his heavy-lidded eyes have to be so darned . . . seductive? She was tempted, very tempted. How easy it would be to go strolling along the river with him and forget about those kids. Nobody else seemed to give a damn. No!

"No!" she said aloud. "I won't be sidetracked. I have work to do. My story."

His brows rose at the vehemence of her reply. "No big deal. Just thought I'd offer." He tossed down the dish towel and left the kitchen, slapping his thigh as he passed Comet. The hound roused and trotted along beside him.

After an hour of unproductive work, Maggie put aside her notes and stood, rubbing the back of her neck. It was too darned quiet. She was used to city sounds, traffic and sirens outside her window, not crickets. And she wondered if her exposé would make a darned bit of difference—if she could get it printed. Her documentation was pretty good, but she'd have to make it foolproof for a publisher—and his lawyers—to take on the story.

She rubbed her neck again, arched her back, and rotated her shoulders to get the kinks out. Having to earn her keep as chief cook and bottle washer in this two-bit operation was taking a big chunk of her time and energy. Writing her series was going to take longer than she'd planned. Thank heavens the weekend wasn't far away. She'd devote those days totally to her research and writing.

In the meantime, she had another problem to cope with—besides the potent distraction of a certain green-eyed conundrum. She hadn't the vaguest idea how to make chicken and dumplings. Her culinary ignorance was such a small concern in the grand scheme of things, but somehow her ineptitude seemed to epitomize her general sense of failure of late. Strange, since she'd been canned from more than one job in her life—usually for her smart mouth and her refusal to conform rather than for incompetence.

Maybe she was simply getting a head start on her mid-life crisis, but she never used to feel so inadequate. The old Maggie Marino was tough. Resilient. Her ex had told her, usually in the heat of one of their endless arguments, that she didn't need anybody or anything. She'd agreed and been proud of it. She'd always made it on her own. She'd spit in the eye of trouble and kept on going.

Why, now, was she feeling so . . . melancholy, so alone?

She'd always been pretty much a loner, and she'd been comfortable with that. Maybe the threats on her life had shaken her more than she'd realized. Maybe she was simply homesick for the excitement and energy of the city, for the familiar. Maybe— Oh the hell with it. All that introspective nonsense was giving her a headache.

After she fixed herself another cup of instant coffee, Maggie wandered to the front door, drawn by the soft sounds of a guitar outside. Telling herself that she only wanted some fresh air, she went out to the porch, leaned against the railing, and sipped from her mug. Shade played softly, smiling broadly when he spotted Maggie, then watching her intently.

Shade noted the rigid way Maggie held her body, and he could almost feel her coiled tension. He would have liked nothing better than to massage her stiff shoulders and kiss the pale skin of her nape.

The dim yellow porch light sparked her hair with bits of flame that reminded him of a campfire on a dark, lonely night. He wanted to warm himself against it, run his fingers through the unruly thickness, and rub it against his cheek, even if he got burned in the process.

Maggie Marino had some soul-deep misery. He knew because his own seemed to call out to her.

She turned. "You play very well."

"Thanks. Have any requests?"

She walked the few steps to where he sat rocked back in a chair, and she sat beside his feet which were crossed with heels resting on the porch rail.

"Whatever you're playing is lovely. But I don't recognize the song. What's the name of it?"

"It doesn't have a name yet. It's not finished."

She looked surprised. "You're writing it?"

"Yep."

"So you're a songwriter?"

"Sometimes."

"What do you do the rest of the time?"

"Oh," he said after a moment's hesitation, "a little of this and a little of that. Lately, as little as possible."

"You don't sound very ambitious."

"Look what happened to Caesar."

She gave him a saucy smile. "Sid?"

He laughed. "Julius."

They lapsed into an easy silence as he

continued to strum the half-formed song. He watched her as she stared off into the darkness of the woods beyond the cabins, and he could feel an almost palpable sadness emanating from her. The feeling found its way to his fingers. Mournful strains floated from his guitar into the stillness of the night.

Her eyes shimmered with sudden moisture, and he saw her jaw tighten.

"Want to talk about it?" he asked quietly.

She shook her head.

"Need another hug?"

Her gaze locked with his. Her eyes blazed momentarily, then softened. She nodded.

Shade set aside his guitar and stood. "Come here."

He held open his arms, and she slid into them as if they were a perfect fit. He hugged her close, then continued to hold her, thinking that it felt so damned good that he'd hold her all night if she'd let him. Fearing to break the spell, he said nothing. He merely stood there with his arms wrapped around her, his only movement a faint brushing of his chin against the top of her glorious mop of silky copper-colored hair.

He felt himself growing aroused and tried to will away the feeling before she became aware of its evidence. He had a hunch that she'd bolt if she knew what was on his mind. As prickly and sassy as Maggie was, she also had a vulnerability that she tried to hide, and it was very close to the surface now. He had to tread carefully.

"Shade?" she murmured into his chest.

"Hmmm?"

"May I tell you something in strictest confidence?"

"Sure."

"I'm really not much of a cook."

He dared not laugh. "I sort of figured that."

"Could I ask you a favor?"

"Name it and it's yours." Hell, if she'd asked him, he would have waded into the Neches River and caught an alligator with his bare hands.

"Would you teach me how to make chicken and dumplings?"

He grinned as he rubbed the top of her head with his cheek. "You betcha."

She pulled back enough to look up at him and smile. "Thanks."

"You're very welcome. You don't ask for help much, do you?"

She shook her head.

He smiled. "You should try it more often. You might be pleasantly surprised."

He bent to give her a friendly peck, the seal of a bargain between friends. But her lips were so soft, so warm, so alluring that he couldn't pull himself away. Nor did she make any effort to stop him.

Something almost magical seemed to meld them together, to part their lips and increase the pressure. His tongue found hers, and the kiss deepened with an intensity that sent shock waves through him. It seemed crazy, but he felt as if he'd been waiting a lifetime for that moment.

FOUR

Maggie hummed as she pinned back her hair with combs.

"You certainly seem happy this morning," Omie Nell said, turning off the vacuum cleaner.

Maggie grinned. "Maybe the country air agrees with me." She applied her makeup while Omie Nell chattered about her boyfriend, Billy Earl, who was in college at Texas A&M. They were "sort of" engaged, secretly. It seemed as though Omie Nell's parents weren't nearly as fond of Billy Earl as she was.

"He's going to be home on break this weekend. We'll be at the dance Saturday night. 'Course I have to work part of the time, but you can meet him."

"What dance?" Maggie asked.

"Oh, there's always a dance here every weekend—with a band and everything. Everybody comes to Buck's on Saturday night. They get down and *rowdy*! You wouldn't want to miss it."

Maggie didn't express her profound disinterest in getting down and rowdy in a backwoods beer joint. "Mmmm," she said instead.

"Billy Earl is a terrific dancer. I can hardly wait until tomorrow. It seems like forever since I've seen him." The young blonde stared off into space, starry-eyed.

"Tell me, Omie Nell, where can I find a decent library around here? I need to do some research . . . for my book."

"I suppose the best one is at Lamar University where I go to school. Their library is pretty good, and Beaumont is only about half an hour away if the traffic's not bad. I just think it's wonderful—about you being a writer and all. I absolutely love mysteries. Agatha Christie is my favorite. Is your book going to be anything like hers?"

"Uh . . . not exactly."

Maggie got directions to the campus from Omie Nell. Then she tried to work for a while, but her mind seemed sluggish this morning. Unusual, since, as a reporter, she'd learned long ago to tune out everything and focus totally on the story she was writing. But her thoughts were determined to wander to Shade. She kept finding herself staring off into space, looking, she was sure, as starry-eyed as Omie Nell.

His kiss had thrown her for a loop. She couldn't remember when a simple kiss had affected her so. Scratch simple. There had been nothing simple about it. She'd turned into a mindless puddle. If a kiss could do that to her, she wondered—

Dammit, Marino, get hold of yourself or you'll be in a bigger mess than you're already in.

With the greatest of effort, she managed to subdue her thoughts enough to make some progress before it was time to begin lunch. She was *not* going to allow herself to go all gaga over an ex-marine with no name or visible means of support . . . even if he could quote Shakespeare and kiss like a dream. She'd talked to her uncle Silas's attorney about selling the property, and as soon as her exposé was finished, she was out of this backwater burg, she reminded herself as she headed for the tavern's kitchen.

Using Shade's suggestion from the night before, she mixed the leftover hash with the last of the lemon-basil mushroom soup and added a couple of cans of tomatoes, one of beans, and a few extra spices. The mixture, which didn't look half bad and smelled surprisingly good, was bubbling on the stove when Shade walked in holding a squawking chicken by its feet.

"What in the world is that?"

He grinned. "It's a hen."

"I *know* that. What are you doing with it here?"

"We're going to make chicken and dumplings, and Mama always said that a fat, fresh hen made the best ones."

Maggie looked at him in horror. "But it's *alive.*"

"Yep. I just bought it from Prentis Newton down the road. He said it was a good fat one, and there's no question that it's fresh."

She cocked an eyebrow. "Feathers and all?"

"You'd have to dress it first."

"Why do I have a feeling that you're not talking about putting it in a little pinafore and sneakers?" When he laughed, she said, "If you think that I'm going to whack that chicken's head off and shave the feathers, you're out of your ever loving mind."

"Pluck."

"Pardon?"

"You don't shave off feathers; you pluck them."

She waved her hand in a dismissive gesture. "Semantics. I've never killed anything bigger than a cockroach, and I'm *not* into chicken plucking."

"And you don't chop the head off; you wring—"

"Spare me the details." She wrinkled her nose and shivered at the thought. "Get it out of here. Looking at its beady little eyes gives me the creeps."

To her relief, Shade, his shoulders shaking suspiciously, left with the squawking, flapping chicken. Fifteen minutes later, he sauntered back into the kitchen.

"Is the dastardly deed done?" she asked.

He shrugged. "Nothing to it. I—"

She held up her hand. "I don't want to discuss this."

He laughed, caught her around the waist, and pulled her to him. "Ah, my Maggie, you're not nearly as tough as you make out."

Her breath caught as she looked up at him. His eyes were shining with merriment in a way that she'd never noticed before. He kissed her quickly and moved away, grabbing plates and utensils to set the table.

She touched her lips briefly, then turned to prepare the grilled cheese sandwiches.

As they were finishing their lunch, which Buck had complimented profusely, a rangy, tanned man in a straw hat came in the tavern door. He held a package wrapped in newspaper.

Shade jumped up quickly and intercepted the man, taking him outside to talk.

Puzzled by Shade's strange behavior, Maggie asked Buck, "Who was that man?"

"Prentis Newton. Lives up the road a piece."

"What was in the package?"

Buck shrugged. "Probably that hen Shade bought."

"I thought he was going to dress it himself."

"Shade?" Buck guffawed. "Hell, I doubt if he'd know which end to start on. He's used to—" He cleared his throat. "That was a mighty fine meal, Miss Maggie. Mighty fine. I can hardly wait to taste them dumplings."

Later when she was washing dishes, Shade fell into his easy habit of drying them. Casually, she said, "Explain to me how you go about plucking a chicken."

"Oh, I wouldn't want to make a city girl like you squeamish by relating the details." A grin played around the corners of his mouth.

"Try me."

"Well, there are all sorts of methods, I suppose. It's a matter of individual style."

"What style do you prefer?"

"Paying Prentis five dollars to do it."

"You faker!" She laughed and flung a handful

of soap foam at him. "Why did you bring that live chicken in here anyway?"

Laughing, he looped his dish towel around her waist and pulled her to him. "Because I like to see your eyes shoot sparks. Did you know that they glimmer like sunlight on polished amber?"

She draped her arms over his shoulders and said playfully, "I love it. Tell me more."

As his eyes searched her face, their laughter slowly died. The merriment in his gaze shifted into a smoldering intensity that stunned her.

Lightly grazing her cheek with his knuckles, he said, "Your skin is like translucent alabaster." Dipping his fingers in her thick, curly hair, he lifted it and sifted strands through his fingers. "Your hair is like . . . words fail me."

She laughed nervously and glanced away. "How about a mess? I keep thinking I'll cut it off, but I never seem to have the time."

"Don't. It's . . . a whirlwind of silken fire. Like you."

Ordinarily, she would have laughed, thinking such comments corny, a mawkish flattery obviously designed for prurient purposes. But his words and the mesmerizing depth of his eyes stirred a rippling thrill over the surface of her skin, and the soft rumble of his voice reverberated deep inside her. Half-frightened by the potency of her reaction to him, she pulled away and turned back to the sink. "For someone whose words fail him, you do very well. You must be part Irish. With a glib tongue like yours, I'll bet you drive the women around here wild."

"Maggie—"

He'd spoken her name sharply, and when she glanced at him with a feigned guilelessness and lifted her eyebrows in reply, she could see that a muscle worked in his jaw. "Yes?"

"Have you ever caught a crappie or catfish on a cane pole?"

"I've never caught any kind of fish on any kind of pole. What's a crappie?"

"I can see that your education is sadly lacking. Let's put the hen on to boil and go fishing."

"But I need to work this afternoon."

"Working on a beautiful day like today would be a sin against nature. There's a nice breeze on the river, and I hear an old channel cat calling my name."

"You must be having auditory hallucinations because I don't hear a thing. I need to work on my story. Like some people I know, I can't spend my life loafing."

"Ah, Maggie mine, you're a tough lady to get around. You want me to teach you how to make dumplings? You'll have to come fishing with me first."

"That's blackmail."

"Yep."

"Are you sure this thing is safe?" Maggie asked, eyeing the green flat-bottomed boat tied at the riverbank.

"I'm positive." Shade deftly stepped into the boat and turned to give her a hand.

She stepped in gingerly, then squealed as it rocked precariously. She had visions of ending up in the muddy water with snakes and alligators.

Laughing, he held on to her. "It won't tip over. Trust me."

"Trust you? I don't know you well enough to trust you. How can I trust someone who won't even tell me his name? You're so secretive about your past that for all I know you could be an ax murderer."

He didn't answer, but he gave her the strangest look.

"You're not . . . are you?"

He chuckled. "An ax murderer? No."

He helped her don a life jacket, then retrieved their gear from the bank, untied the boat, and shoved off. She sat in the front, facing him, while he eased into the back. Instead of starting the motor, he let the current carry them downstream, using a paddle to keep them on course.

She tried to keep her gaze on the pastoral scenery, the winding river, blossoming branches, the multishaded green hues of trees that stretched as far as she could see. Central Park would have been lost in the vast expanse surrounding her. She tried to focus on the rippling water, the aquatic insects skimming its surface, and the iridescent-winged dragonflies that flitted, hovered, then flew away. She made a conscious effort to observe these things. But her gaze returned again and again to the man in the boat.

He wore a pair of threadbare jeans that stretched tightly across his thighs—and very nice thighs they were. Tucked into the waistband was a faded black shirt that had probably once been a jersey. It looked as if he'd converted it into a tank top by shearing deep armholes with hedge trimmers. On anyone else, the clothes would look sloppy. On him, they looked . . . very sexy. Especially when he raised his arms and the tattered garment displayed the sides of a muscled upper torso and a glimpse of extraordinary pecs.

As he dipped the paddle into the water, she became fascinated by the powerful play of tanned biceps, of sinewy arms stroking, stroking. The flower-entwined cobra that circled his upper arm expanded and contracted with his movements, making the snake appear alive. It seemed both deadly and alluring. She'd never noticed before that the cobra's eyes were the same green as Shade's. Raw power seemed to emanate from both man and serpent. It wrapped around her, swelled her breasts, and tightened her belly.

"See something you like?"

She felt a quick flush spread up her throat. "I'm interested in your tattoo. What kind of flower is that?"

He glanced down as if he'd forgotten it was there. "Belladonna."

"Belladonna. Deadly nightshade. Is that why you're called Shade?"

He shrugged. "I was nineteen, drunk, and feeling my oats. It's nothing. I guess I should see about having it removed."

"I like it."

One side of his dark mustache twitched, and he winked at her. "Then I'll leave it."

"Oh, don't do it on my account," she said quickly. "I mean, in a few weeks I'll be . . . I mean . . . oh, look, there's a rabbit."

He didn't turn to look. He only smiled in a way that made her extremely uncomfortable. "There are lots of rabbits around here."

They continued on in silence for a few minutes. Again she looked at the trees, the river, the sky, to seek out the birds whose calls filled the woods around them. She closed her eyes and tried to concentrate on the warm, earthy smells of the river, spring vegetation, and clean air. But her eyes popped open and her gaze slid to his hands and their grip on the paddle. No sissy hands these. He had big hands with broad palms and long fingers. She wondered if they were callused and how their roughness would feel against her skin.

"What are you thinking?"

His husky voice startled her, and her eyes met his. He knew what she was thinking. Damn him, he knew.

"I . . . I was just wondering why you aren't wearing a life jacket. You insisted that I put one on."

"I like to live dangerously."

There was a hint of humor in his words, but there was something else as well. Something that made her shiver. His comment, the tattoo, his reticence to discuss his past—

"I can almost see the wheels turning in your pretty head," he said. "Out with it."

"Is it your experience in Vietnam that makes you the way you are?"

"How am I?"

"You don't seem to have much ambition beyond hanging around Buck's, drinking beer, playing pool, strumming on your guitar, or helping me cook. You won't share anything of yourself. You are so secretive . . . so"—she fluttered her hands— "I don't know exactly how to describe it. I have a strong feeling that you're hiding something. Or maybe repressing it. Vietnam vets often have trouble reintegrating themselves into society."

He chuckled. "I appreciate your concern, Maggie, but I dealt with my Vietnam experiences a long time ago. It wasn't pleasant, but I don't have flashbacks or nightmares. I'm not suffering from post-traumatic stress syndrome. I'll admit that I had some trouble for a while, but unlike some of my buddies, I had a strong support system and a loving family. But even though I've dealt with it, I still don't like to talk about it."

He seemed to have pat answers for her questions, and if he didn't want to discuss it, she knew better than to press him. Still, she wondered about his behavior, his peculiar reluctance to talk about himself. "Tell me some more about your family."

He paddled toward the bank and tied the boat to a willow branch that hung over the water. "My father died several years ago. My mother is a wonder. She loves to garden, volunteer at the hospital—" He grinned. "And she's a fantastic cook."

"And your brothers? What do they do?"

"Oh . . . they own a ranch, among other things."

"With horses?"

He laughed. "With horses." He handed her a pole and dipped his hand into a bucket near his feet. "Want me to bait your hook?"

"I'm no sissy. I can bait my own hook."

He held out his hand to her. A tiny silver fish flopped in his palm.

"What's that?"

"It's a minnow."

"But it's alive."

"Of course it's alive. How else would it attract the fish?"

She took the wiggly thing in her hand and tried not to make a face. "What do I do?"

"Stick the hook through the middle. Here." He pointed to a spot.

She tried. She really tried, but it was harder than she thought. To do the vile deed, she screwed up her face and closed her eyes, but she kept missing. The last time she tried, she snagged her jeans.

When she opened her eyes to free the hook from the fabric, Shade was watching her with a puzzled expression. "What are you doing?"

"Baiting my hook."

"You're doing a lousy job. It would help if you kept your eyes open."

She gave him a haughty look. "You do it your way, and I'll do it mine."

Shade hung his head, and a burst of laughter exploded from him, shaking his shoulders and rocking the boat. "Ms. Maggie Marino, for all your sass, you're nothing but a cream puff." He deftly slipped the bait on her hook.

She stiffened her spine and glared at him. "I am *not* a cream puff. Just because I don't enjoy poking sharp things into helpless minnows and chopping off chickens' heads doesn't make me weak. And, Mr. Macho Ex-Marine, I noticed you weren't so quick to kill that hen yourself. Now what do I do with this damned hook?"

"Toss it over the side and hold the end of the pole. Like this." He demonstrated, and she imitated his actions.

"Now what?" she asked.

"Now we wait. Be quiet and watch your cork."

She watched the red-and-white cork float on the river's surface and waited thirty seconds. A minute. Two minutes. Nothing happened. "Why am I watching the cork?" she whispered.

"When a fish strikes, he'll take it underwater."

She waited a couple of minutes longer. Still nothing happened. "Is this supposed to be fun?"

He grinned. "Be patient."

"I don't think I'm cut out to be a fisherperson. Patience has never been my greatest virtue. Maybe my minnow escaped." She lifted her line until she saw the tiny silver fish wiggling at the end, then plunked it back into the water. The two-toned bobber floated a moment, then went under. "My cork! My cork!"

"Set the hook!"

She glared at him. "And exactly how do I set a hook?"

"Too late. He's gone."

"Well, damn!"

"He probably took your bait with him."

Sure enough the hook was bare. She grabbed a minnow from the bucket, said, "Sorry, fellow," and impaled him on the barb.

She didn't allow herself to think again that the minnow reminded her of a goldfish she'd once had—the only pet she'd had as a child. How thrilled she'd been over that goldfish. She'd proudly carried him home to their apartment in a small plastic sack of water. She'd changed the water in his bowl faithfully; she'd talked to him and sprinkled food in every morning before she left for school. Goldie hadn't lasted long either. He'd gone belly-up six weeks after she got him. She'd cried for days. That had been the year that her mother had died.

Tossing her hook out into the water, she sighed, prepared for a long, boring wait. Almost immediately her cork disappeared under the water.

"I've got another one!" she shrieked, giving the pole a smart yank.

Shade grinned with pure delight, watching Maggie's animated face as they walked back to Buck's. No, he walked; she almost danced on air, bubbling with excitement over the three fish she'd caught. He loved the way she laughed and smiled with that lush, generous mouth. Her vivacity spread across her entire face in an undisguised, contagious merriment that lit up her surroundings and warmed his insides. Most of the women he'd known seemed to think an honest guffaw was unfeminine or that a big grin might crack their makeup.

Maggie smacked her fist into her hand. "Boy, did you see that catfish fight? But I landed that sucker. How much do you think he weighs?"

He held up the string of fish. "Oh, about two and a half pounds. Are you going to clean these?" Her smile died, and he could have kicked himself.

"I'd forgotten about that."

He hooked his arm around her neck and kissed her nose. "I could be persuaded to do your dirty work for a price. How about going into town with me after supper? There are a couple of movies I've been wanting to see."

"Would you take a rain check? I have to get some notes organized before I go to Beaumont tomorrow. I plan to spend the day researching at the university library."

"Sounds dull. Why does a mystery writer have to do research?"

"Oh . . . I need to check some facts about my setting. And find out the effects of certain poisons. Lots of things."

"Need some help?"

She shook her head. "Thanks anyway." She grabbed his hand. "Come on. I want to show Buck my fish."

He held up the string of two crappie, which were barely keepers, and one decent eating-sized catfish. "You're really tickled about these, aren't you, squirt?"

She pulled in her chin and tried to restrain her smile. "Yep."

He laughed at her imitation of him and squeezed her hand. He couldn't remember when he'd had more fun—and he'd barely dipped his own hook in the water. Her excitement over each fish was like a kid's with a Christmas toy. Maggie Marino had brought renewed zest into his life and nestled next to his heart without even trying. He felt as if he'd spent his entire existence simply marking time, waiting until she walked into Buck's, looking like a drowned rat and acting as feisty as a cornered fox.

Long ago he'd grown weary of flawlessly coiffed and designer-dressed women who only saw dollar signs when they looked at him. His ex-wife was a perfect example, and he was lucky to be rid of her. Maggie, with her gutsy, vibrant personality, and the endearing vulnerability she tried so hard to camouflage, was tailor-made for him. And as far as she knew, he didn't have the proverbial pot. . . . Now if he could convince her that they would be perfect together, his life would be complete.

He'd learned quickly not to crowd her or push her. He would bide his time, tether her loosely and give her the illusion of room to run, but he meant to have her. And he always got what he wanted in the end.

As they neared the bait shop, Shade spotted a candy-apple-red pickup parked by the door and uttered a silent curse. He might be mistaken, but he had a hunch who the driver was. Dammit! He wasn't ready for this.

"Looks like Buck has a customer," he said, steering Maggie toward the cabins instead of the shop. "I'll put these on ice, and you can show him later."

She balked. "But—"

"And we need to get cleaned up and see about the chicken. It ought to be about ready by now."

Shade knew he was talking too fast and practically dragging Maggie to her cabin, but he'd be damned if he'd let anybody screw things up now.

Maggie thought Shade's behavior extremely suspicious. He was obviously trying to steer her away from whoever was with Buck. Why? Her reporter's antennae went up.

In record time, she showered, dressed, and headed for the tavern as fast as her size-ten sneakers would carry her. She noted that the red pickup was still there and went in the back door of the kitchen. She eased into the tavern, positioning herself in the shadows where she could see through the bait-shop doorway and not be seen.

Buck was talking to a big, tall man, about Shade's size and build, who wore a black cowboy hat, boots, and something else that startled her. He had a silver star pinned to his vest and a gun strapped to his belt. His hat was pulled low on his forehead above dark eyebrows and sin-black eyes.

Too far away to overhear their conversation, she eased closer, plastering herself against the wall next to the open door, and eavesdropped shamelessly.

"Are you sure you haven't seen him?" the man in the black hat asked.

"Can't say that I have," Buck replied.

"Now you wouldn't lie to a Texas Ranger, would you, Buck?"

"Are you callin' me a liar?" Buck sounded angry.

"Hooo-wee, partner, don't get your hackles up. I'm just mighty anxious to find him. This is serious business. There might be a sizable reward for any information on his whereabouts."

"You want me to tell you what you can do with your reward?"

"You're a true-blue friend, Buck, but I aim to find him. And soon."

"I wish you luck."

The Ranger laughed. "I'll bet you do. Much obliged anyhow."

Judging that the conversation was over, Maggie hurried back to the kitchen and peeked out the window as the truck drove away. As soon as the dust trail was out of sight, she saw Buck hurry to Shade's cabin.

Peculiar. Very peculiar.

Had they been discussing Shade? Granted, she'd only heard the end of the conversation, but if they had been talking about Shade, why was a Texas Ranger looking for him? She was bursting with a dozen questions.

In a few minutes, Shade joined her in the kitchen. He had changed clothes and his hair was still damp. He didn't look particularly nervous. In fact, he was his usual laid-back self. She opened her mouth to question him, but closed it when she realized that she couldn't ask the things she wanted to know without revealing that she'd been eavesdropping. She decided to wait and pump Buck later.

"Are you ready to get this show on the road?" he asked.

"I'm ready. What do we do first?"

The two of them made a great team, and in no time they had made and rolled out dough, cut it into strips, then slowly dropped the thin pieces into the boiling chicken broth. With Shade coaching, they cooked a big pot of black-eyed peas and one of turnip greens, which didn't seem at all appetizing to her, and made a pan of crusty corn bread, which smelled heavenly.

While they were setting the tables for their usual trio and for a pair of fishermen who had arrived earlier, her nagging curiosity could be tempered no longer. She said casually, "I noticed that the man with the red truck that Buck was talking to earlier wore a gun and a badge. Who do you suppose he was?"

Shade shrugged noncommittally. "Might have been a game warden. They keep pretty close tabs on fishing and hunting violations around here."

A game warden. Of course, she thought, feeling silly. He must be like a park ranger. When she'd heard him say, "Texas Ranger," she'd thought of the Texas Rangers in the old western movies. They'd probably disappeared with the horse-and-buggy days.

Shade stopped at the door of her cabin, and said, "Dinner was a roaring success. I do believe those were the best chicken and dumplings I've ever eaten."

"They were good, weren't they? Buck must have liked them too; he ate three helpings. But you and your mother's recipe deserve all the credit." After a quick kiss on the cheek, she murmured, "Thanks."

He gave her a devilish grin. "Is that little peck all I get for slaving over a hot stove for hours? Come on, you can do better than that."

He gathered her in his arms and brought his face close to hers. Her eyes closed automatically. She waited. He didn't kiss her. Her eyes opened. "What are you waiting for?"

"For you."

Damn him for making her take responsibility! She almost pulled away and left him standing there with that smug look on his face, then thought, *I'll show you, buster!* She planted a fervid, openmouthed kiss on him designed to melt his boot heels.

Her plan backfired. From the moment that their lips met and his tongue plunged into her mouth, she was the one who went up in flames. His hands stroked her firmly, scorching the skin beneath her clothes, then slid to her bottom and pulled her closer to his searing hardness.

When a deep growl from his throat resonated in hers, fire flashed through her, heating her blood to such a point that she was sure her shoestrings had disintegrated and her rubber soles were welded to the concrete.

FIVE

When the alarm went off Saturday morning, Maggie groaned, batted the snooze bar, and rolled over. Hadn't she closed her eyes only moments before? It *couldn't* be time to get up. She opened one bleary eye to look at the clock and groaned again.

Flinging the covers aside, she thrust herself from the nice warm bed, grumbling that she deserved to do penance for allowing thoughts of a man to keep her nerve ends tingling and her body tossing most of the night.

Furious with her ridiculous behavior, she forced her fractious flesh to stand under a cool shower—not cold, she wasn't that much of a masochist—before she allowed herself a cup of coffee.

After jump-starting her brain with a shot of

caffeine and filling Byline's food bowl, Maggie dressed comfortably for a day at the library. Two whole days to work undisturbed!

"Think of it, Byline," she said, scratching the cat's head, "two whole days when I don't have to look at a pot or a pan or an uncooked pea!" She gave him a final pat. "I'm leaving plenty of food and water in case I'm late getting back." She gave him a jaunty salute, picked up her satchel of notes, and was off.

The station wagon's engine caught right away and ran smoothly along the highway to Beaumont. Following Omie Nell's directions, she easily found the university library.

Inside, a friendly student assistant showed her around and helped acquaint Maggie with the systems. Pleased with the facilities and the computer network capabilities, she soon lost herself in research. She might be a lousy cook, but Maggie Marino darned well knew how to ferret out a story.

And what a story it was turning out to be! As she traced information on Tree Hollow's board of directors, she became more and more excited. After only preliminary examination, she'd found that a couple of them had a few rattles in their closets. She strongly suspected that when she dug deeply enough, she'd find sufficient old bones to supply every biology class in the country.

Most of the kids who sought haven at Tree Hollow needed help to avoid drugs, sex, crime, and violence—not to be exploited and encouraged in those very directions. They needed role models, not ones who were bent on lining their greedy pockets or indulging their perversions. And she was determined to strip those depraved miscreants down to their cadaverous ugliness for violating the guardianship of Tree Hollow and its kids. To hell with their threats!

When the announcement of the library's closing at five penetrated her concentration, she was disappointed. But as she stood and stretched the kinks from her back, she realized that she'd been working for eight hours with only a bathroom break. She was famished.

Reluctant to return to Buck's, she asked the student assistant to recommend a good restaurant.

"Do you like Cajun food?"

Maggie shrugged. "I've never eaten it, but I'm game."

"Hebert's is a cozy little family restaurant that serves some of the best gumbo and étouffée in town."

"Sounds good to me."

After securing directions, she drove directly to Hebert's. As she parked she noticed a bookstore a few doors down and decided to pick up a paperback novel to enjoy with her dinner.

A bell on the door tinkled as Maggie walked in, and an attractive blond woman behind the counter looked up from the book she was reading and smiled. "Hi," the woman said, giving the word three syllables in typical Texas fashion. "Welcome to The Great Escape. May I help you with something?"

Maggie decided on the latest mystery by a well-known authoress she'd been meaning to read.

She'd paid for the book, walked back to the restaurant, and was opening the door when she noticed a candy-apple-red pickup truck enter the parking lot near the bookstore. She almost backtracked to see who was driving, then shrugged and continued inside. A coincidence, she told herself. She'd seen dozens of red pickups that day. It seemed as if every other person around here drove some kind of truck.

Dinner was delicious, especially since she didn't have to cook it, and she'd enjoyed the quiet corner where she'd read the first two chapters of the mystery she'd bought. The novel was a compelling story about a woman who fell in love with a charming, sexy man who, unbeknownst to the heroine, was a hit man. And that premise started her thinking again about Shade. She'd learned long ago that the world was populated with crazies, and what did she really know about the man who claimed only one dubious name?

Of course she wasn't in love with Shade, but she was fast becoming emotionally entangled with him. And who did she know to vouch for him except Buck? And what did she know about Buck except that he was the owner of a beer joint and a man she'd never heard of until a few days ago?

Texas, she was sure, had as many crazies as New York, but she'd allowed slow Texas drawls and good ol' boy manners to anesthetize her brain, lull her into a comfort zone. A certain savvy and a healthy dose of cynicism had helped her survive in a tough world. She was a fool if she abandoned those traits now.

Back off, babe, she told herself. Getting overly involved with Shade could be bad news.

It was almost eight when she reached Buck's. Cars and trucks were everywhere and more were arriving as she pulled behind the main building and into her parking space. A blast of loud music from the tavern hit her when she opened the car door. As she rounded the rear of the wagon, she saw Shade coming through his cabin door with an armload of clothes.

Her defiant heart skipped a beat, and she felt a momentary panic.

Grinning broadly, he approached her. "Glad to see you back safe. Did you have a productive day?"

She took a deep breath and smiled politely. "Very productive, thank you. Are you leaving?"

He winked. "Not a chance. My bathroom developed a plumbing problem, and I'm moving next door." He gestured with his head to the cabin on the other side of hers.

"Need some help?"

"This is the last load," he said, "but I'd be much obliged if you'd get the door for me."

She hurried to open the door, and as he strode through, she turned to leave.

"Don't rush off yet. Come on in. I want to talk to you."

Despite all the self-castigation about crazies that she'd indulged in on the way from Beaumont, she stood there like a panting puppy, waiting. She wasn't sure what it was about Shade, but the moment she came into his presence, her head always lost in the conflict with her heart. Whether it was his easy smile, his hypnotic eyes, or the smooth way he carried his body—or all of those things—she didn't know.

He hung up his clothes and quickly shut the closet door. "It's stuffy in here." He raised the window in the kitchenette that was a clone of hers, then walked to where she stood. He looked especially handsome in jeans with a crisp crease, ostrich boots, and a Native American-patterned western shirt with pale green stripes that enhanced the color of his eyes. He was freshly shaved, his mustache trimmed, and he smelled of a rich scent which she vaguely recognized as one of the expensive men's colognes.

He kissed her briefly. "I missed you today." He brushed her hair back and scanned her face, then frowned. "You look tired."

"I am." She shrugged her shoulders, trying to ease their tightness.

"Turn around." He shifted her until her back was to him and began kneading her neck and shoulders with his strong, sensitive fingers. "Have you had dinner? Hershel Vick and his wife take care of the food on weekends, and his barbecue is the best I've ever eaten."

"Thanks, but I had dinner in Beaumont." Having someone recognize her tiredness and care if she'd had dinner gave her a warm, comforted feeling. And having someone who could give such an exquisite back rub was heaven. She moaned at the delicious magic he worked on her aching muscles. "If you were a millionaire, I'd marry you tomorrow."

His fingers stilled. "A millionaire? Is that the kind of man who interests you?"

She laughed. "Lord, no. That was simply a figure of speech. Deliver me from tycoons. I had one of those already, and one was enough for me."

He resumed massaging her tense muscles. "Your ex-husband was a millionaire?"

"Not while we were married, but he was well on his way. The last I heard, he'd made it. I'm happy for him, and even happier that I don't have to be a part of that scene."

He worked his thumbs slowly up the sides of her spine, and her back arched with the delicious sensation. Just as she was about to become a boneless puddle, he swatted her bottom and stepped away. "Why don't you go take a nice, relaxing bath, put on some jeans, and we'll go boot scootin'."

"Boot scootin'?"

"Country-and-western dancing. Can't you hear the music?" He hunched his shoulders, swayed, and snapped his fingers to the tempo.

"Only a deaf person could miss it. I don't have any cowboy boots, and I don't know how to 'boot scoot.' "

He gave her a cocky grin. "Well, Maggie mine, you're about to learn from a master."

"I'm really very tired. I think I'll take a

shower and curl up with a good book in bed."

"Need some company?"

"No, thanks. Why don't you run along and scoot your boots with somebody else."

He sobered. "There is nobody else."

Something in his expression melted her heart and shot her resolve to smithereens. "I may be over later."

"Yeee-haaa!" came the shouts over music that bounced off the ceiling and vibrated the floorboards under Maggie's feet. Raw energy crackled through the packed room of wall-to-wall people who were laughing and talking, drinking beer, and dancing. Maggie didn't see Shade, not that he would have been easy to spot through the haze of smoke and the flailing maneuvers of gyrating bodies.

She pushed her way to the bar and found Omie Nell, who was pulling a shift as cocktail waitress and about to hoist a tray of long-necked bottles and frosty mugs.

"Hi!" Omie Nell said with a perky bobble of her blond curls. "I'm glad you decided to come. Isn't this great?"

"Ask me again when the culture shock wears off. Is your boyfriend here?"

"Oh, yes. That's Billy Earl over there." She

pointed to a tall, skinny boy with a huge Adam's apple who wore a wide-brimmed black cowboy hat resting low over his jug ears. "Isn't he dreamy?"

"Mmmm," Maggie mumbled in lieu of the truth. To each his own, she thought as she perused the long-legged dancer who sported a faded circle in the back pocket of jeans which barely hung to his scrawny hips. "Who's his dance partner?"

"That's his sister, Mavis. She's going to relieve me in a few minutes." An ear-splitting whistle from one of the tables cut through the noise, and Omie Nell laughed. "Let me deliver these beers before Lester raises a ruckus."

Buck was busy behind the bar. When Maggie caught his eye and waved, he drew a draft and set the mug in front of her. "On the house."

"Looks like you're busy tonight," she said.

"Get most of my business on Saturdays. Especially when Shade's around."

Puzzled by his comment, she asked, "Why then?"

"He always plays a couple of sets, and folks love him." He gestured with his head toward the other end of the room where the band and dance floor were.

She turned to look just as the foot-stomping song ended and a slow ballad began. A guitar around his neck, Shade stood at the microphone.

When he began to sing in a deep, rich voice, she heard a collective sigh around the room. As she watched him and listened to the song, his rumbling, mellow tones vibrated low in her belly. His words about looking for a woman to love and the sonorous timbre of his voice caressed her, sent thrills over her body, made her breath catch. Sensuous, scintillating, seductive—none of the terms adequately described the effect.

"He's fantastic, isn't he?" Omie Nell whispered, adding a little sigh. "*So* talented and *so* sexy. Did you know that he writes all his own music?"

"I'm shocked," Maggie said. "I had no idea."

"He could put his boots under my bed anytime." Omie Nell sighed again. "It's a pity I'm not older." She gave Maggie a pointed look and a suggestive smile.

Maggie watched Shade pour out his emotions and play the audience like a pro. She was as spellbound as the others. For a moment, she was sure that he'd spotted her and was singing only for her. When the last note died, she felt captivated, enthralled . . . drained.

After only a two-beat pause, he and the band cut loose with a fevered country rock song that sent the house wild with whistles, cheers, and stamping boots. With that wicked grin of his and several suggestive moves, he looked straight at her and belted out a sexy lyric about a "red-hot woman with red-hot eyes and a red-hot mouth that is just my size."

With the heavy beat of drums and bass added to his gravelly growl and the jerk of his shoulders and hips, the song hit every one of her erogenous zones. Her belly contracted; her breasts plumped; her nipples constricted.

"Oh . . . my . . . God . . ." she said, staring at Shade and holding on to the bar as her knees buckled.

"Isn't he incredible?" Omie Nell yelled over the din of music and shrieking women.

"Incredible is too mild a word."

"Red-hot, she's red-hot," he sang.

He winked at her, swiveled his body, and delivered dynamite-charged verses designed to inflame. His performance worked for her.

For the first time in her life, Maggie understood why frenzied women tossed their panties to singers—or tried to tear off the performer's clothes. Pure primitive instinct. She could feel her own revving up. Her upper lip grew damp. Her shirt stuck to her back.

"I love it when she's *red*-hot." His eyes on her, he grinned and made a pelvic rotation to a drum riff that would have put Elvis to shame.

Burning up and sure that she was about to hyperventilate, Maggie pushed her way through the steamy, smoky room that was closing in on her and out into the cool night air. In a shadowed area away from the building, she leaned her forehead against a pine tree and sucked in deep breaths.

What was happening to her?

Hell, she admitted, she knew what was happening to her. Shade had turned her on like crazy. She'd never had a man affect her so profoundly. And with just a song and a look. Holy Moses.

After another few deep breaths and a great deal of self-admonishment about her juvenile reaction, she regained control of her rampaging emotions and her intellect kicked in. The more she discovered about Shade, the more confused she became.

Exactly who was this man?

She'd first thought him uneducated, unsophisticated. She'd discovered that didn't seem to be the case. For all his folksy ways, he had a very literate vocabulary. From their conversations, she'd had hints that he was well-read, well-traveled, and astute. Although she was no musical expert, he was obviously enormously talented.

Why wasn't he recording in Nashville or, at

least, playing in an urban area where he could make a name for himself?

Was he in hiding? Why?

"Maggie!" a female voice called from between the parked cars.

"I'm here, Omie Nell."

"Oh, thank heavens," the young woman said. "You took off so fast that we were worried about you. Shade sent me to check and see if you're all right. He was coming himself, but the crowd nearly revolted when they thought he was going to leave."

"I'm fine. I guess the smoke got to me."

"Are you coming back in?"

Maggie shook her head. "I'm very tired. I think I'll go to bed."

"Oh. Okay. But I think Shade's going to be very disappointed."

Omie Nell turned to leave, but Maggie called her back. "Answer one quick question for me. What do Texas Rangers do?"

"You know, I'm not exactly sure, but I believe that they're involved with investigations and catching criminals. They're real tough customers, I know that."

Her answer startled Maggie, but she managed a smile. "Thanks. See you later." She waved and headed for her cabin.

A dozen explanations came to mind as she

walked toward her door, but one kept pushing ahead of the others and clamoring in her mind. Her strong hunch was that the Texas Ranger she'd seen yesterday had been looking for Shade. Why?

What was he running from? Why was he hiding? But he wasn't really hiding, was he, if he performed for a hundred or more people? What did all this mean?

She examined every possibility she could think of from his being in the witness protection plan to being a fugitive wanted for murder. Damn it all, she was going to find out!

And she knew exactly how to start.

In her cabin, she changed into a dark sweatsuit and sneakers and dug around in her belongings until she found a small flashlight. Byline twined around her ankles, meowing, and padded beside her as she went to the door.

"Stay here," she told him, but as she went out, he scooted through the crack and ran into the night. "Stubborn cat," she muttered.

Checking to see if everything was clear—and it was—she loped around to the back of the cabins until she found the open window in Shade's kitchenette. It was a bit too high for her to climb in easily, so she shone the flashlight around, looking for something to stand on and wishing for a ladder. The beam settled on some sort of box contraption made of boards and wire. She dragged it to the cabin wall and carefully stepped up on it. It was rickety, but it held well enough for her to hoist herself up and through the window.

Once inside, she climbed down from the counter, then let out a muffled curse when she barked her shin on a kitchen chair. The porch light filtering through the curtains and a small slit where they didn't close completely provided a faint illumination, outlining furniture and casting shadows, but not enough to see well. She fished the pencil flash from her waistband and shone the beam around the room. It stopped at a chest of drawers, and she moved quietly to examine its contents. Starting with the bottom, she found only clothes and ordinary odds and ends—including a full box of condoms, she noted—until she came to the top drawer.

Underwear. Briefs. Silk, she thought, rubbing the fabric between her fingers, and very, very skimpy. An odd choice for someone who wore faded jeans and tattered shirts. As she searched under the neat stacks, the penlight captured a glimmer of gold. She looked closely.

A Rolex watch. And it wasn't one of those phony copies that hucksters all over New York City peddled to unsuspecting tourists. This one was eighteen-carat gold.

Curious. Very curious.

She closed the drawer and went to the closet. There was the expected assortment of jeans and shirts, but in the very back, she found a suit. She checked the label and frowned. Armani.

Several pairs of boots and shoes neatly lined the floor—including an exceptionally expensive brand of Italian wing tips.

In a far corner of the closet, half-hidden by a duffel bag, she spotted a hand-tooled leather briefcase. She knelt down and dragged it toward her.

A key rattled in the cabin's door lock, and her heart leapt into her throat. Dear Lord, she couldn't let him find her here! She shoved the briefcase back in the closet and considered her options in a flash.

She scrambled across the room and dived under the bed just as the door swung open.

She held her breath as two pairs of boots—one large, one small—entered the room. She heard a male's low whisper and a female's soft giggle as they walked toward the bed and stopped. They stood toe-to-toe.

Maggie's eyes widened in horror as she watched the small boots leave the floor and heard the unmistakable sounds of kissing. Low male murmurs, moans. Female sighs.

That bastard!

When the mattress sagged and the springs creaked above her head, she almost suffered apoplexy. Dear Lord, surely she wouldn't be forced to endure—

An empty boot hit the floor. Then another one. Two more thunks followed until four boots lay helter-skelter in her line of vision. When she heard the sounds of zippers, giggles, and more deep-throated moans, and when she saw clothes landing in scattered heaps on the floor, she had a perverse urge to jump up and yell, "Surprise!"

Of course she couldn't. She could only continue to stay sprawled under the bed. She closed her eyes and covered her ears, trying not to play the voyeur, but when the bed began to bounce vigorously, her eyes flew open, and she sucked in a horrified gasp.

Humiliated beyond description by her predicament and having to listen to Shade's grunts and groans as he made it with one of his groupies, she cursed her fate and cursed the man. She called him every vile name she'd ever heard and strung together profane invectives in new and creative ways.

When the bed stopped bouncing—after what seemed an eternity—she slumped from tense exhaustion, her cheek against the floor. Her nose tickled. Dust. Omie Nell hadn't been as thorough with her cleaning as she should have been.

"Ohhhh, babe," he groaned.

"Ohhhh, sweetlips," she sighed.

Ohhhhh, Lord, Maggie thought.

An awful vision flashed through her head. What if they stayed in bed all night?

Suddenly, her nose tickled in earnest, and she had the overpowering urge to sneeze. She inched her hand up, pinched her nostrils, and fought the sensation with every bit of determination she could muster. She began to pray as fervently as she'd ever prayed in her life that they would go back to the tavern.

The powers that be smiled on her. The urge to sneeze passed, and the libidinous bed-bouncing duo began gathering their clothes and dressing.

Maggie waited a full minute after they left before she crawled from under the four-poster. Her first impulse was to escape immediately, to run like hell for the sanctuary of her cabin. But some diabolic sense of justice made her linger.

Justice, hell. Vengeance! She wanted *revenge* on the glib-tongued son of a bitch who'd sweet-talked her into thinking that he cared for her, who'd kissed her as if she had been special, who'd kept her tossing in her bed at night.

Eyes narrowed, she considered a variety of schemes before she settled on her plan. With a devious, witchy giggle, she rubbed her palms together and went to work.

SIX

When the band stopped for a break, Shade said, "I'm going to pack it in and leave it with you guys."

"You're not going to finish the night with us?" asked Pete, the bass player.

"I must be getting too old for this. I'm worn-out."

Pete, who was at least ten years older than Shade, guffawed and slapped him on the back. "Sure you're not cuttin' out to meet one of them hot-to-trot fans of yours behind the bushes? I could name a dozen lovely ladies who're ready and willing."

"Nope. Not interested."

Shade made his way through the crowd, declining to linger and socialize with several who encouraged him, some rather emphatically since the hour was growing late and the alcohol consumption had risen to a point where inhibitions were being cast aside. He tried to be accommodating, especially with the ladies, but he really didn't enjoy their fawning over him.

Outside, he breathed in cool, clean air to clear his head as he walked toward the cabins. He got a kick out of performing his own music and playing a couple of sets with the band occasionally, but he'd discovered that he wasn't cut out for a steady diet of that sort of life. The idea of rowdy crowds and an entertainer's life on the road didn't have the appeal that he'd once dreamed it would. He could finally relegate his interest in music to its rightful place as a hobby and be content, in a bittersweet sort of way, with the decision.

He was sorry that Maggie hadn't stayed. He'd wanted to dance with her and ask her how she'd liked his songs. A couple of nights ago when he hadn't been able to sleep for thinking about her, he'd written "Red Hot."

He wondered if she realized that he'd written the song with her in mind. Obviously she didn't appreciate his music, since she'd left in the middle of the number.

He hesitated at her door for a moment, then moved on when he noticed that her cabin was dark.

He unlocked his door, pushed it open, and turned on the light.

"What the hell!" he roared.

Toilet paper streamers and two condoms, inflated like balloons, hung from the ceiling light. Other uninflated condoms were brandished on various protuberances in the room, including one sheathing each of the bedposts.

Cursing, he stripped the decorations from the display and strode to the bathroom to dispose of them. When he saw what was on the medicine cabinet, he let out another string of oaths. Written in blue toothpaste across the mirror was a terse gutter admonition followed by three exclamation points.

Who had vandalized his room? Kids on a dare? An irate boyfriend irritated about his girl's reaction to Shade's performance?

Burglars?

He couldn't imagine burglars taking time to hang streamers or blow up condoms, but he checked his belongings to be sure. Nothing significant was missing. He noticed the open window in the kitchenette, slammed it down, and locked it.

Still rankled about what he'd decided was a kid's prank, he took a quick shower and got into bed.

He felt a rip as he thrust his feet under the cover.

Damn! He hadn't been short-sheeted since he and his brothers were kids at camp.

Ten minutes after Maggie returned to her room, she regretted her adolescent reaction— not that she wasn't still furious, she was. But ordinarily she handled her anger in a more adult fashion. What was it about that man that made her behave in totally alien ways?

Determined to excise the philanderer from her life as much as possible given the circumstances, she left the cabin early on Sunday morning and drove to Beaumont. By wandering around the museums, having lunch, and buying two Southern-style cookbooks, she killed time until the library opened at two, then stayed until closing at eleven. She wouldn't be able to avoid him completely, but she would keep as physically and emotionally distant as she could.

Shade was totally bewildered. He'd missed seeing Maggie Sunday, and when he entered the kitchen on Monday to help her with lunch, he felt as if he'd opened the door to a meat locker. The look she gave him was glacial. When he tried to touch her, she shrugged his hand away.

"What's wrong, Maggie?"

She didn't look up. "I'm busy."

"Need some help?"

"No. Why don't you go shoot some pool, play your guitar, or do something equally constructive. Out of here."

"Are you angry about something?"

"Angry? Why should I be angry?"

He shrugged. "Damned if I know, but you act like you've got a burr under your blanket. Is it that time of the month or something?"

Eyes shooting familiar sparks, she whirled on him and held up the butcher knife she was using. "If you value that manhood you like to flaunt, you'd better take your sexist remarks and your butt out of here."

Understanding the wisdom of a tactical retreat, he left, but he didn't have the foggiest notion what he'd done to get her dander up.

During lunch, she avoided looking at him or speaking to him, and when he offered to help her with the dishes, she declined his assistance.

Dinner was no better. She was decidedly cold. Trying to make conversation, he asked, "Maggie, did you hear any commotion in my cabin Saturday night?"

He felt six inches shorter from the cutting

look she gave him. "Was there a commotion? I was sound asleep."

He shrugged and let it go.

The week dragged on miserably with Shade trying to figure out what had happened between them. He tried to talk to her. He got nowhere. He was walking on eggshells, trying to make sure he didn't get her even more riled, but her responses were terse and frosty. Even Buck was growing uncomfortable with the strained atmosphere.

By Thursday afternoon, he'd had enough. He'd been patient; he'd been polite. All he'd gotten for his consideration was frustration. If any other woman had treated him the way Maggie had, he'd have told her to kiss off. But Maggie was worth fighting for—even if she was the one he had to do the fighting with.

He hitched up his jeans, strode to her room, and banged on the door. When she opened it, he shoved his way inside. "All right, Maggie, let's have this out. I want to know what in the hell is eating you."

She glared up at him. "I have nothing to say to you. Please leave."

"I'm not leaving until you talk to me. I thought we had something going for us, and—"

"There is no *us*."

"That's a crock, and you know it. Are you

going to tell me what I've done to set you off? I've tried to think of anything I might have done to offend you, and I can't come up with an answer unless my performance with the band Saturday night bothered you. Is that it?"

"If you enjoy having women screaming and swooning while you shake your pelvis in their faces, who am I to care?"

For the first time in days, Shade felt a glimmer of hope. "I'll be damned." He smiled and reached for her. "You're jealous."

"Jealous?" she shrieked. "Why, you egotistical, overgrown bum, I wouldn't be jealous of you if you were the last man in the solar system!" She tried to pull away from him, but he held on to her.

"Hell, Maggie, I was just having a little harmless fun. Those women don't mean anything to me. *You* do."

"Harmless fun? Harmless fun?" she sputtered. "You insensitive . . . exploitative . . . *jerk!*" She pounded on his shoulder with her fist. "Let me go. I'm not going to get in line behind a gaggle of groupies to share your bed!"

"What in the hell are you talking about? I haven't shared my bed with any groupies."

Maggie, her eyes blazing fury, whopped him on the shoulder again. "On top of everything else, you're a liar!"

Totally bewildered by her behavior, he said, "I don't know what kind of garbage somebody has been feeding you, but—"

"Nobody has been feeding me anything. I saw you. Me. With my own eyes."

"Exactly what did you see?"

"You and a woman. In your room. Saturday night."

"Honey, you're mistaken. Somebody got in the window and—"

"Not in the window. Through the front door. With a key. I'm not mistaken. I know what I saw. If you don't let me go and get out of here this very minute, I'm going to call the police and press assault charges."

Stunned by the fierceness and irrationality of her anger, Shade left. What was wrong with her? Either she had a serious mental problem or she'd seen something and misinterpreted the facts. He preferred to think the latter.

Nobody had a key to his cabin except . . .

Two hours later, Maggie was still agitated. She tried to work, but her mind kept replaying the scene with Shade. She tried to read, but when she discovered that she hadn't comprehended a single word, she tossed the book aside and paced.

She asked herself why she cared what a man

she'd only known a few days did in the privacy of his bedroom. A couple of kisses, no matter how steamy, was nothing. Nothing.

Why had she allowed herself to become so worked up over a shiftless womanizer whose only effort at anything like gainful employment was playing once a week in a backwoods beer joint and who was probably running from the law?

Someone knocked on the door. Sure of whose big knuckles were pounding the wood, she ignored it.

The knocking grew louder, more insistent.

Byline started yowling.

Maggie flung open the door, set to give him a bigger piece of her mind.

Omie Nell stood there with Shade. Her face was pale, her eyes big.

Shade marched the girl into the room. "Omie Nell has something to tell you."

"I—I—" The young blonde looked from a stony-faced Shade to Maggie, then down at her hands, which were laced together in a white-knuckled grip. "I thought the room was empty."

Maggie frowned. "What are you talking about?" She glared at Shade. "What have you done to her?"

"Oh, no, he hasn't done anything to me. He—he—that is, I—I—I mean, Billy Earl and I used his room Saturday night. Shade's room, that is, but it wasn't his usual room. We didn't know he'd moved. I thought it was empty, and we wanted some time together, and, oh, I could just die," she said in a rush.

Maggie looked from Shade to Omie Nell, who had turned from pale to crimson and was studying her feet. Maggie put her arm around Omie Nell's hunched shoulders. "There's no reason to be upset. It was an honest mistake." She glared at Shade. "How could you humiliate her this way, you bully?"

"Humiliate *her*? Hell, I'm the innocent party in this mess. If you hadn't jumped to the wrong conclusions, we wouldn't have a problem. Couldn't you have trusted me a little? Couldn't you have asked me?"

"Asking you questions is like spitting in the wind."

"Could I go now?" Omie Nell asked in a small voice.

"Certainly," Maggie said. "Shall I take you home?"

"I'll do it," Shade said. To Maggie, he added, "We need to talk after dinner. Buck said to tell you that there'll be four extra."

When the door closed behind them, Maggie sank to a chair, her knees wobbly and her emotions muddled. She would have to apologize to Shade, of course. But she'd also have to come up

with a damned good explanation of how she'd
come to be in his cabin . . . *hidden* in his cabin.
She'd avoided the issue while Omie Nell was
present—offense was always the best defense—
but she was sure that Shade wouldn't ignore
it.

Apologizing, as much as the idea chafed
her pride, wasn't the primary issue. Neither
was explaining about sneaking into his place.
If she were brutally honest, she'd admit that
she'd jumped on his indiscretion as an excuse
to withdraw from him. Her growing feelings for
him had made her extremely anxious. Now that
her shield of righteous anger had been stripped
from her, she had nowhere to hide. She dreaded
their after-dinner talk.

And she hoped that the condom adornment
of his room didn't come up. Chinese water torture wouldn't make her admit that she'd done
such a childish thing.

Dinner! She glanced at her watch, then
grabbed one of her new cookbooks, and dashed
to the tavern kitchen. With four extras, she'd
have to double the meat loaf.

When Shade had dried the last dish and Maggie had wiped the clean counter for the third time,
he said, "Let's go for a walk."

"Wouldn't you like another piece of pecan pie first?"

"No, thank you. It was excellent, but the two pieces I had was plenty. We need to have that talk."

"This isn't a good time for me, Shade. I need to work tonight."

"Maggie." His inflection and the stern look he gave her indicated that he knew she was using delaying tactics.

She sighed and stripped off her rubber gloves.

With his hand at the small of her back, he guided her out the rear door. They walked toward the river where frogs and crickets were tuning up as dusk settled. A slight breeze stirred the woodland foliage and carried a spring-fresh scent that reminded her of a newly cut melon. Although the temperature was mild, Maggie shivered.

"Cold?"

She shook her head. "Nervous."

"You don't ever have to be nervous around me."

Her short laugh had a hollow ring. They walked on silently toward the soft rush of the river. She kept waiting for the ax to fall, but he was as mute and stoic as one of the tall pines beside the trail. He wasn't going to make this easy.

"I might as well get this over." She sighed deeply. "I am truly and profoundly sorry."

"About what?" he asked casually.

"About *what*?" She rolled her eyes. "You know damned well about what."

"Why don't you tell me."

She heaved an exasperated breath. "I'm sorry that I falsely accused you of taking one of your groupies to your room and to your bed. Not that it's any concern of mine what you do, of course, but—"

"Maggie," he interrupted, "look at me." He lifted her chin and gazed deeply into her eyes. "I want my behavior to concern you. Yours concerns me. From the first moment I saw you, thoughts of another woman have been the farthest thing from my mind. My head is full of you. I think about you all day long, and dream about you at night. I'm obsessed with your hair." He threaded his fingers through the thick mass. "With your soft skin." He brushed the backs of his fingers against her cheeks. "With red-hot eyes," he murmured as he kissed each eyelid, "and a red-hot mouth that's just my size."

His lips touched hers and her knees turned to shifting sand. She caught hold of his upper arms to keep from sliding to the ground, and she felt the heady tensing of his big biceps.

"I dream," he murmured in his gravelly voice, "of touching you here." His palms slid over the contour of her hips and bottom. "And here." His hand slipped between them and stroked across the fullness of her breasts in a figure eight that he repeated over and over. "The only woman I want in my bed is you."

She went absolutely boneless as his mouth closed over hers in a soul-stealing kiss that set her afire. Shamelessly she rubbed against him, scrabbling with hands and body to get closer, to climb into his skin. She would have flung her clothes in the river and made love with him on the sandy banks if he hadn't pulled away.

"Do you want me as much as I want you?" he asked, his voice husky with desire.

"Lord, yes."

"I'm not talking about a quick roll in the hay, Maggie. I'm talking serious business here."

She stiffened in his arms.

He sighed. "That's what I thought. Take a little time. Think about it."

She thought of little else.

That night she tossed and turned; the next morning she paced. Preparing lunch, she barely caught herself before she added a pinch of sugar to the Irish stew and a cup of salt to the banana pudding.

Shade, who was helping, chuckled, nibbled

her nape, and nipped her earlobe as he whispered, "Distracted, are we?"

If she hadn't been before, she was then. In spades. "You're making me nervous again. You're looming."

"Looming?"

"Yes, looming. Even when you're not around, you're around."

Encircling her waist from behind as she stirred the stew, he rubbed his face in her hair. "Sounds like you didn't get much sleep last night either. I lay in my lonely bed and thought about you all night long, wishing you were next to me, aching to hold you and touch you." Keeping her close against him with his left arm, he nuzzled her ear and made long, slow strokes down her thigh with his right hand.

Her fingers clutched the spoon in a death grip and her head fell back against his shoulder. "Why are you tormenting me this way?"

"Because I want all of you."

"You're asking too much. How can I allow myself to become involved with someone I know almost nothing about?"

"What do you want to know?"

"Everything."

His hand moved to stroke the front of her thigh. "I'll make you a deal. Once a day you can ask me any personal question you want, and I'll answer it, if you'll allow me to do the same."

"You'll answer truthfully?"

He chuckled. "Yep."

"What's your name? I don't mean Shade. I want to know the name your mother calls you."

"Paul."

"Paul," she repeated, trying out the sound of it. "That's a very nice name. What's the rest of it?"

"Uh-uh. That's two questions."

She stiffened. "You rat!" She tried to pull away but he held her fast.

"You made the deal, darlin'. Now I get my question." He rubbed his cheek against her unruly curls and slid his hand around to her inner thigh. "Is your hair the same glorious color everywhere?"

She dropped the spoon, and it disappeared into the deep, bubbling pot of stew.

After dinner that evening, Shade cajoled Maggie into going to a movie with him. When he'd looked at her with those eyes and said, "Pretty please?" she'd melted, as usual. She didn't know exactly what it was about him that made saying no so darned difficult. If she could bottle it and sell it, she'd soon own Japan.

They drove to the small town nearby, and he bought tickets to a film they'd agreed on. Usually she adored Mel Gibson, even if he was short, but she couldn't keep her mind on the movie. She was too aware of the tall man sitting next to her. His frame was too big for the small space allotted for theater seating, so his leg rested against hers, sending a throbbing awareness from his flesh to hers.

His arm stretched along the back of her seat, and his thumb absently stroked the cap of her shoulder with a message that smacked of proprietorship louder than if he'd shouted it. The scary thing was, the feeling excited her.

She jumped up. "I'm going to get some popcorn."

"Darlin', I have about a half-gallon right here." He held up the huge bucket that they'd been sharing.

"I—I like mine hot."

A slow grin spread across his face. "Me too."

Maggie fled to the ladies' room. There she splashed water on her face and held her wrists under the running water. She wasn't sure how the wrist business was supposed to help calm her, but she'd seen it done often on TV and in movies. All it did for her was get her watch wet.

She dried her face and glared at her reflection in the mirror. When did she lose control here?

Why was she allowing Shade to lead her around by her hormones? Unless he was the greatest actor since Barrymore, his libido was firing on all cylinders as well.

It was time for her to take the offensive. If he wanted to play games, she knew a few moves of her own.

Armed with a fresh bucket of popcorn and a cola, she slipped back to her place. "I brought you a cold drink," she whispered, handing him the cup.

"You didn't get one for yourself?"

She smiled sweetly. "We'll share." She discarded the old popcorn and balanced the new bucket on his lap, then curled up in her seat half facing him and draped her arm on his shoulder. With her index finger, she twirled a lock of hair at his nape, then leaned close to guide his hand so she could sip from the cola, wiggling to make sure that her breast brushed back and forth on his arm.

She smiled; he smiled.

Her breast still pressed against him and her finger slowly drawing a trail to his ear, she slipped off her right Loafer and began to rub his calf with her toes. She felt his body tense, and she bit back a chuckle.

Her eyes on the screen, she patted around on his lap as if reaching for the popcorn and missing. He flinched, then grabbed her hand and stuck it in the bucket.

She smiled; he smiled.

"Thanks," she said, grabbing a huge handful. Half the kernels spilled from her fist. "Oops," she whispered innocently, then dumped the handful back into the bucket and began retrieving the stray pieces from between his thighs. When her fingers chased a particular kernel well up to the juncture of his legs, then lingered as if she had difficulty recovering it, he clamped his hand over her wrist.

"What the devil are you doing?"

She fluttered her eyelashes. "Trying to pick up the popcorn I spilled. I wouldn't want your jeans to get all greasy."

"They're going to be worse than greasy if you keep that up. Let's get out of here."

"But the movie isn't over."

"Who cares? I don't have a clue as to what's been happening on the screen. Do you?"

She shook her head.

As they exited the movie, he thrust the popcorn bucket and the soft-drink cup into her hands. "Hold these while I drive home. If your hands are full, maybe I won't wrap the truck around a telephone pole."

She gave him a smug grin. "What's the matter, big guy?"

"You know damned well what's the matter."

"Uh-huh. You can dish it out, but you can't take it."

"Maggie mine, there's a simple solution to this problem."

"Yep." She laughed and threw the cup and bucket in a trash can by the curb.

Shade broke several speed limits on the way back to the cabins.

When they arrived at her door, he raised her chin and kissed her softly. "Have you thought about what you want?"

"Yep." She grinned. "A *lot*." She grabbed a fistful of his shirtfront and pulled him down to her so that she could reach his lips.

SEVEN

Saturday morning Maggie threw her hairbrush against a wall. The cat jumped a foot, then ran under the bed.

"Sorry about that, Byline. It's just that Shade—Paul—whoever he is, makes me so darned mad, I could explode."

She'd spent another restless night. And just because she wouldn't say the magic words he was waiting for. To make matters worse, he was right. Despite the perpetual state of lust that Shade aroused in her, she'd never been one for casual sex—certainly not in this day of AIDS and other sorts of disease. Frankly, she'd never considered herself a particularly passionate woman. But she'd undeniably had her fuse lit.

Although she wasn't suited for one-night stands, neither was she ready to make any sort of long-lasting—or even medium-lasting—commitment to a mystery man. Indeed after snooping in his cabin, she didn't know any more than she had before. Her finds only raised more questions. Why a Rolex watch and an Armani suit? What had he done before he moved into a dinky cabin near the river however many months ago? He must have earned a living somehow.

The questions continuing to swirl in her head, she grabbed her satchel of research notes and her bag and went out the door.

Shade sat on her porch, his chair balanced on the back two legs and his feet propped on the railing. He smiled. "Good morning. I didn't want to knock in case you wanted to sleep in. How would you like to drive down to Galveston and spend the day?"

She shook her head. "Sorry, I need to work at the library in Beaumont."

"Need any help? I could go along and turn the pages for you."

"I can't handle the distraction."

A slow grin creased the brackets along his cheeks. "Not even if I promise to be on my best behavior?"

"Not even then." She started to the wagon, then remembered something and turned back to him. "I get another question today, don't I?"

"Yep. Me too."

Considering her choices carefully, she finally asked, "What did you do for a living before you came here? Did you play in a band?"

"Well," he said, leaning against the porch railing, "I've worked at lots of things, but I never played in a band. Always wanted to, but I never did. Let's see . . ." He stroked his mustache with his index finger and gazed upward as if thinking. "I've done a little bit of everything including working on an oil rig in the Gulf and branding cows. And I've tried my hand at insurance, real estate, and a couple of other things. I've written a few songs that never sold. And . . . uh . . . did I mention the banks? That's mostly what I did."

She squinted at him. "*You* worked in a bank?"

He shifted his feet and, Maggie noted, acted decidedly uncomfortable. "Well, I didn't exactly work *in* the bank. I wasn't a teller or anything like that."

"Were you a guard?"

He cleared his throat. "I guess you could say I was a sort of guard. I kind of looked after things. That's over your limit for today. I counted about four questions."

He was embarrassed, she thought, which was silly . . . but very endearing. Being a bank guard was a perfectly honorable occupation. "I'm sure you did well with whatever you turned your hand to."

He shrugged. "I didn't have any complaints."

She smiled. "And about my extra questions, I'll owe you."

As she turned to leave, he said, "Whoa, squirt."

She waited patiently while he walked to her and draped his arms over her shoulders. "Ask away."

"What size shoes do you wear?"

She stiffened. "Never ask a woman her shoe size."

He cocked a dark brow. "You welshing?"

"Of course not, but it's a strange question. Are you insinuating that I have big feet?"

He laughed and kissed her nose. "Darlin', beside my size fourteens, yours are down right dainty. Now are you going to tell me?"

"Very well," she said huffily. "Nine and a half narrow." That was close enough, she thought, and none of his darned business anyway.

He softly brushed his mouth against hers, once, twice, teasing her mercilessly, making her lips tingle and pucker wanting more. Much more.

"Sure you don't want to play hooky and go to Galveston with me?" he asked, then brushed her lips again. "I'll buy you a humongous cone of pink cotton candy that will tickle your pretty nose and melt like sweet fairy wings on your tongue."

"Sweet fairy wings? How poetic."

"I'm a poetic kind of guy." He closed his eyes, wrinkled his face like a blues singer, and snapped his fingers. "Got rhythm and romance down deep in my soul." When she snickered, he grinned. "Tell me the truth, how long has it been since you've had cotton candy?"

"A long time," she said wistfully, faintly recalling a time from her meager repertoire of happy childhood memories. "You tempt me, but no. I have to go to the library."

"Don't get too tired out. I'm planning on dancing with you tonight."

"I've told you that I don't know how to do all those country-and-western dances. Anyhow, I have two left feet."

He glanced down at her sneakers. "Looks like one of each to me. You obviously haven't had a good instructor. I'll have you two-stepping in a flash."

"Are you going to perform too?"

A slow lopsided grin, with a decidedly lascivious insinuation, spread over his face. "I might be persuaded under the right circumstances."

She rolled her eyes. "I meant with your guitar on the stage."

"Will it bother you if I do?"

Oh, it would bother her all right. The same as it would bother every other female who was under the age of ninety and still breathing. "I suspect that your fans would riot if you didn't."

"That's not what I asked. Say the word and I won't."

"I have no right to tell you what to do."

He leaned his forehead against hers and said, "Maggie darlin', I'm offering you that right."

He kissed her gently, and she became totally flustered. "Play, by all means, play. Sing your songs. No sweat. It's fine with me. I have to go." She broke away and hotfooted it to the car before she agreed to give him her firstborn child or anything else he requested.

Lord, the man's eyes were lethal. And his deep, husky voice was the essence of auditory seduction.

Maggie had a phenomenally productive day at the library. She worked furiously for eight hours following thread after thread until she was positive she had everything she needed for the exposé that would lead to a real investigation by the police. Now all she required was a couple of corroborations and a few uninterrupted days to write the piece. For the former, she would call someone in New York who owed her a few favors and get some help with verification; the latter was more of a problem with Shade around.

Having worked through lunch again, she stopped by the same restaurant, Hebert's, for another meal of the Cajun food she was learning to adore. Maggie complimented the proprietor so profusely that she left with several recipes, including one for gumbo that she was sure she didn't have the patience to make from scratch.

As she walked to her car, she happened to glance toward the bookstore she'd visited the week before. A red pickup was parked in front, one with an extravagant amount of chrome and a roll bar. She hadn't thought of the Texas Ranger in several days, but seeing the red truck reminded her that the one he'd driven had those same gaudy accessories.

Another coincidence, she told herself. But her ingrained tendency to snoop propelled her toward the bookstore. A "Closed" sign was on the door, but the lights were on. On a pretense of perusing books in the window display, she casually looked inside the shop.

Her heart began to pound at a furious rate when she saw a tall, black-hatted man locked in an amorous embrace with the blond owner.

Dear God, it was the Ranger! Maggie turned and quickly walked to her car.

It wasn't until she was behind the wheel that she realized how foolishly she'd acted. There was no reason to feel like a cookie thief. The Ranger didn't know her from Adam, and she didn't have so much as an outstanding parking ticket.

If she really wanted to know if he'd been looking for Shade, and why, Fate had dropped the perfect opportunity into her lap. All she had to do was go back to the bookstore, tap on the window, and beg to make a fast purchase. Using her ditzy redhead routine, she could strike up a conversation and pump him. She had a gift of gab that had left a trail of closemouthed types shaking their heads and wondering why they had spilled their guts to her. Shade had been the irritating exception to her technique.

She opened the door and had one foot on the pavement when something stopped her, a reluctance totally foreign to her.

Did she really want to know?

How stupid! Of course she wanted to know.

But her body stayed as stuck to the seat as if she'd been sitting in a giant wad of chewing gum. Shade's lazy smile flashed in her mind, and she could almost hear his low voice saying, "Trust me, darlin'."

She argued with herself until the moment was lost. Doors slammed, an engine revved up, and the red pickup roared from the parking lot.

"Damn!" She slammed her fist on the steering wheel. What was happening to her? The Texas sun must have fried her brains. Or maybe all that flour she'd inhaled in the kitchen had turned to mush in her head.

She chastised herself all the way back to Big Bucks. It was becoming a familiar routine.

When she arrived at her door, she found a large box wrapped in pricey paisley foil and topped with a big red bow. "What in the world?" She picked it up and took it inside with her.

Byline twined around her legs as she dumped her satchel and purse on a chair and the mysterious gift on the coffee table. She bent to scratch the cat's ears. "Did you miss me or are you hungry? No, don't answer that. I'd only get my feelings hurt."

She toed off her sneakers, plopped down on the couch, and eyed the fancy package. "Now what do you suppose that is? My birthday isn't for months yet."

"Meow."

"Good idea." She slipped off the bow and ripped away the paper. Inside the package was a magnificent pair of boots in a vibrant rust color. Giddy with delight, she ran her fingers over the buttery soft eelskin and inhaled the rich aroma of new leather. A card was tucked between them. The note written in a bold hand said:

> *Boot scootin' is easier if you have boots.*
> *Meet you on the dance floor.*
>   *Love,*
>   *Shade*

She hugged the boots to her. Nobody had ever given her a "no-occasion gift." Certainly not one so obviously expensive. She ought to return them, but she rubbed her face against the soft leather and knew that she couldn't part with them.

A sudden, horrible thought struck her. She checked the printing on the end of the box and groaned.

She crossed her fingers and prayed that the boots ran long.

They didn't.

It was God's retribution for her little white lie. She'd only shaved off half a size when she'd reported to Shade, but, oh, what a difference that tiny bit made to her big toes.

Her toes be damned! She'd rather be drawn and quartered than admit her duplicity. So, freshly showered and primped, wearing jeans, the thinnest pair of socks she owned, and her new boots, she set out in the direction of the wall-vibrating noise.

The moment Maggie pushed open the door, Shade spotted her. Damn, she was gorgeous. Her hair was a wild, fiery mane and she wore an aqua sweater and tight jeans molded to a figure that made his palms itch. She stood at the entrance and looked around, then spied him and smiled. When she started toward him, he felt his jean placket tighten. He took another swig from his beer, set the bottle on the bar, and stood waiting for her.

"Hi," she said, stopping in front of him. She glanced down at her feet, then back at him, and her smile broadened into one so dazzling that he wanted to kiss her right there, right then, in front of God and everybody. "Thanks for the boots. I love them."

"Do they fit okay?"

"Like you wouldn't believe." She laughed and tossed her head so that her hair moved in a feathery curtain of sparks. He ached to put his arms around her and bury his face in the silky curls.

"You want to dance?" he asked.

"I'd rather have a drink first and work up to it gradually."

She slid onto the bar stool next to his, and he motioned to Buck. "What would you like to drink?"

"I'd like a nice Chablis, but I'll settle for a beer."

He grinned. "Watch me work magic." He'd heard her mention the night before that she liked Chablis, and while he was shopping for Maggie's boots, he'd picked up a case. He'd put a pair of bottles on ice the minute he got back. When Buck handed him the wineglass, Shade held it out to her. "Voilà."

"How did you manage this?"

"Like I said, magic."

She laughed in that sexy, throaty way that never failed to tease his thoughts with tactile images of cool sheets and soft, warm skin. They sipped their drinks, and he tried to keep up a half-sensible conversation, but all he could think about was holding her in his arms.

When the band started a familiar song, he pulled her to her feet. "That's a two-step and an easy one to learn. Come on."

He guided her through the crowd and onto the dance floor. After a brief demonstration, she caught on to the steps immediately, but even though he adored her, he had to admit that she was not exactly nimble-footed. Perhaps it was the new boots, he thought.

"How do those boots feel?" he asked as they did the slow, slow, quick, quick, sliding steps around the floor with the counterclockwise flow of the crowd.

She missed a beat and looked at him strangely. "Why do you ask?"

"It just occurred to me that you aren't used to them, and I'm probably a fool for suggesting that you wear them dancing without breaking them in first."

She smiled brightly. "No problem, but I can't talk and count at the same time." Her feet faltered as she lost the rhythm. "Rats!"

"You're doing fine, darlin', you're doing fine."

She was dying, in wretched torment.

Maggie had never been so relieved in her life as when Shade had to leave her to play his set. She hobbled to the bar on throbbing stumps. Her feet felt as if they were clamped in a torture device with somebody beating her toes with a sledgehammer. She was bound to have blisters on top of blisters, and she wouldn't be surprised if she lost the nails on both of her big toes.

Had they only been dancing a little over an hour? From the excruciating pain, Maggie could have sworn she'd been stomping around for a couple of days. Shade had taught her how to line dance and polka and boogie, and she'd gamely given her all to every single dance. Of course she would probably have a permanent disfigurement and limp for the rest of her life. How did ballerinas endure such anguish to their extremities?

"You look whupped," Buck said. "How 'bout a glass of that fancy wine?"

"I am whupped. Could I have the bottle?"

"Comin' up."

When he returned, she gulped two quick glasses of Chablis and resisted the temptation to pour the rest of the wine down her boots. She also resisted a third glass. The alcohol hadn't numbed her feet, and it was better to be sober and in pain than tipsy and in pain.

Shade was singing, women were going bananas, and she didn't even care. She wasn't sure she could walk, much less dance anymore. What excuse was she going to give Shade? She'd rather suffer thumbscrews than admit that she'd lied about her shoe size.

She succumbed to temptation and had another glass of wine. What the hell?

It didn't help. Nothing would help until she pulled these bone crushers off her feet.

She propped her elbows on the bar, her forehead in her hands and tried to focus her mind on pastoral scenes, on starry nights, waterfalls, clouds, and waves washing ashore. Her efforts fell flat. After only a second or two, her brain abandoned the diversions and screamed, "My feet are killing me!"

She felt arms go around her waist and a kiss land on the back of her neck. Glancing up to the mirror, she saw Shade's reflection behind her. Wearing a tank top and sleeveless jean jacket and with his hair tousled and damp, he looked sexy enough to pose for Mr. November in a hunk calendar. She knew that every woman in the place envied her, but all she could think of was her feet.

"Ready to boogie some more?" he asked.

Stretching her lips in the closest equivalent to a smile that she could summon, she said, "You betcha. But wouldn't you like to have a cold beer first?"

"Naw. I'd rather slow dance with you. I had the guys play it special."

"Then let's do it." Drawing on the vast supply of Marino gumption, she stood.

Tears sprang to her eyes; her stomach went queasy, and sweat popped out on her upper lip. Her knees sagged, and Shade caught her before she hit the floor.

"Darlin', what's wrong?"

"I'm a little woozy. I must have had too much wine, and it's awfully close in here."

"Let's get you outside for some air."

Leaning on him and wincing with every step she took, Maggie tried not to limp, but she couldn't help herself. By the time she made it to the door her feet felt like those of an inept fire walker standing in a bed of burning coals.

She obviously hadn't fooled him, for he looked at her, distress knotting his face, and said, "It's the boots, isn't it? Dammit! A bowlegged armadillo would have better sense."

She shot him a withering look. "I am *not* bowlegged."

"Oh hell, honey, not you. Me. I'm the only damned dimwit around here. I ought to be cut up for fish bait." He scooped her into his arms and started carrying her toward the cabins.

"Put me down. You can't carry me."

"Looks like I'm doing a pretty fair job of it."

"But I'm *heavy*."

"Naw. I haven't even worked up a sweat yet. Put your arms around my neck and stop wiggling." At the door to her cabin, he said, "Where's your key?"

"Ohhh, dear."

"Oh, dear what?"

"It's in my purse."

"Where's your purse?"

"In my room."

He strode to his cabin and set her on the porch rail while he unlocked the door. Then he picked her up again, carried her inside, and kicked the door shut behind him.

He placed her gently on his bed. "Now let's get those damned boots off and see what kind of damage my stupidity has caused." He lifted one of her legs and started to tug the boot off by the heel.

She couldn't stifle a shriek.

He muttered a string of oaths that was much more colorful than any she'd ever heard. "Darlin', I'm sorry. I'm so sorry." He fished in his pocket and pulled out a bone-handled pocketknife.

Her eyes widened as he unfolded a wicked-looking blade. "What are you going to do?"

"I'm going to cut the damned things off. That's what I'm going to do."

"But my beautiful boots! They'll be ruined."

"I'll buy you another pair."

She winced as he sliced through the exquisite rust-colored eelskin. She desperately wanted relief but she couldn't stand to see something so lovely destroyed. Stupid that she should care if the boots were ruined. She'd have sooner been stretched on a rack than to have crammed her feet into them again.

"Maybe next time I should get a larger size. These seem to run a little short," she said casually.

When he peeled the first boot off, it was like having one foot in heaven. She flopped back on the bed and held up the other leg.

The moment the second one was off, she heaved a long shuddering sigh. "You can't imagine how good—"

He let out another string of oaths, more colorful than the first.

She jerked upright. "What's wrong?"

"You have blood on your socks. Damn it to hell, I ought to be beaten with the bad end of a churn dasher."

She laughed. "I'm not sure what a churn dasher is, but it sounds excessive."

"Dammit, Maggie, this isn't funny." Slowly, he began to remove her socks. "You could get an infection."

"Not likely. I think a blister must have popped." When she looked at her mangled feet, she made a face. "Look gross, don't they? Oh, well, I heal quickly."

Shade muttered another obscenity, then said, "Pull off your jeans, and I'll be right back."

She grinned. "What? No foreplay?"

"Oh hell, Maggie, sex is the farthest thing from my mind right now. I'm going to get a first-aid kit and something for you to soak your feet in. Soaking is easier with your pants off." He strode to the bathroom and came back with a terry-cloth robe. "Put this on if you're modest."

His condescending tone pushed her button, but rather than deliver a scathing retort, she decided to do something devilish. As soon as he left, she skinned off her jeans. *The farthest thing from his mind, huh? We'll see about that.* She peeled off her sweater and tossed it aside. She started to unhook her flower-patterned bra and strip off the matching panties, then thought better of it. That might be too much.

Plumping his pillows into a stack against the headboard, she artfully arranged herself atop his patchwork quilt and waited.

The longer she waited, the more time she had to think. It had been a dumb idea, she decided, and was reaching for Shade's robe when the door opened.

Carrying an ice chest and with a first-aid kit under his tattooed arm, Shade made two steps into the room and froze. His eyes narrowed and his jaw tightened as he stared at her.

"Why the ice chest?" she asked.

He looked down as if surprised to discover that he was holding it. He cleared his throat. "It's for soaking your feet. To help keep down the swelling." He avoided looking at her again as he strode toward the kitchenette. "You might want to put on the robe so you won't get cold."

She almost giggled. Now who was being modest? "I'm very comfortable, thank you." In truth, she was darned uncomfortable, but nothing would have wrung the admission from her.

She heard water running, and in a couple of minutes, Shade came back with the big red chest and placed it near an easy chair. He walked to the bed and scooped her up as if she were no more than a sack of cow feed.

"My feet are much better. A little soap and water and a good night's sleep, and I'll be fine."

"*I'll* be the judge of that."

He set her in the chair and, with the toe of his boot, dragged the chest closer. She looked down at the large insulated container that was half full. "But that's *ice* water. I'll get frostbite."

He chuckled. "Not in five minutes. Trust me on this."

With her instinctively resisting, he firmly grabbed her ankles and plunged her feet into the icy bath. She stiffened, drew in a startled gasp, and dug her fingernails into the arms of the chair. But after the initial shock wore off, she had to admit that the water felt divine to her burning feet.

But her teeth soon started to chatter.

"Cold?" Shade asked.

"Not at all." She managed a tight-lipped smile and clamped her mouth shut.

"You are the most hardheaded creature I've ever met."

She smiled sweetly. "Takes one to know one."

He rolled his eyes heavenward, then stalked to the bed, ripped off the quilt, and wrapped it around her. "Better?"

"Marginally. Is the five minutes up yet? My feet feel like Popsicles."

He fetched a towel, knelt by her, and lifted her ankles onto his knee. He blotted each foot until it was dry. Something about his gentle touch and the tender expression on his face as he dried her feet got to her. A huge lump swelled in her throat. She tried to swallow it down, but it wouldn't budge. Her eyes began to sting and grow filmy. She blinked furiously, but in spite of all she could do, a tear spilled over and ran down her cheek. Cocooned in the quilt, she couldn't free a hand to wipe it away.

Shade glanced up, and his expression went dark. "Oh, darlin', I'm sorry. Am I hurting you?"

She shook her head. When he lifted her foot and kissed her instep, the tears really started to flow.

"Sweetheart, I'm trying to be as gentle as I can."

"I know."

He reached for the ointment from the first-aid kit and carefully smoothed it over the blisters and abrasions, then bandaged her toes and put strips on the back of each heel. When he was finished, he kissed the bottom of each foot.

She sniffed. Oh, damn! Now her nose was running.

His face clouded, his brows drawn together, he said, "Honey, I'm so sorry about those damned boots." He gathered her up and carried her back toward the bed.

She sniffed again. "It's okay. You didn't hurt me. My feet are much better. I can hardly feel them at all."

"Then why are you crying?"

"I'm not crying. I never cry."

"Maggie. There are tears rolling down your cheeks. I think *Webster's* defines that as crying. Why?"

He kissed her forehead, and the waterworks began in earnest. She leaned her head against his shoulder. "Because nobody has ever taken care of me like you do."

"Maybe that's because nobody has ever loved you like I do."

Her heart did a somersault. "You can't love me."

He looked amused. "I can't?"

"No. You haven't known me long enough."

He put her down on the bed so that she was propped against the pillows. Bracing himself on the mattress, he leaned over her and kissed both eyelids, then her nose. "Maggie Marino, I've loved you all my life. It just took me a while to find you."

Shade started to move away, but Maggie scrambled from the confines of the quilt and grabbed a handful of his jean jacket.

EIGHT

"Damn you, Shade, you can't just drop a bombshell like that and then walk away. Explain yourself." She tugged on his jacket until he sat on the bed beside her.

He shrugged. "What's to explain? I'm in love with you. Damned if I can tell you how it happened. You walked into Buck's, and I felt as if somebody had clobbered me with a Louisville Slugger. I'd like to marry you."

"Marry me?" she shrieked. "You don't know me."

"I know enough. I knew right away that you were the one for me."

"But that's impossible. There's no such thing as love at first sight. That's romantic drivel. I dated my ex-husband for *two years* before we got married."

Shade smiled. "And how did that work out?"

"That's beside the point."

"Is it? Did you love him?"

"I thought I did," she mumbled.

"How did he make you feel?"

"That's personal."

"What about our deal? I answered all your questions this morning, and you owe me a couple more."

How had John made her feel? She had to think for a while to come up with an honest answer. "He made me feel less . . . well, at first he made me feel as if I sort of . . . belonged somewhere."

"How did it feel when he kissed you?"

"Pleasant."

He snorted. *"Pleasant?"*

"Yes, pleasant. You've had your questions. Now we're caught up."

He gathered her into his arms and kissed her with an openmouthed fervor that almost sent her through the ceiling. Her toes curled, her back arched, and she moaned into his mouth as his tongue boldly danced against hers.

"How do you feel when I kiss you?"

"Breathless," she whispered raggedly. "Hot."

"Darlin', you don't know hot yet."

One corner of his mustache lifted in a sexy smile that sent chill bumps racing over her skin. Without taking his eyes from her, he yanked off his boots and tossed them in a corner, shucked off his jacket and sent it sailing across the room. He popped open the top button of his jeans and moved toward her like a stalking panther.

Her temperature went up ten degrees just watching him. "Aren't you going to turn off the light?"

He slowly shook his head and sat down on the mattress facing her. "No way. I want to see you."

His gaze and hers followed his left hand as it traveled in a lingering path up the outside of her leg from ankle to hip, then slipped to the front of her thigh. Her breath caught as his thumb moved, lightly stroking the sensitive inner curve before his hand slid slowly back down to her ankle. He repeated the action, his right hand joining in to caress the other leg when he reached her knee on the upward stroke.

"I love your legs. So long and perfect. I dream about them wrapped around my waist."

Her heart almost stopped with his words, then began beating violently as both thumbs grazed spots maddeningly close to a place that had gone damp with desire.

He bent and kissed her belly button, and her stomach contracted abruptly when he circled it with his tongue. He chuckled and the sound vibrating against her skin sent thrilling ripples up her torso.

His lips and tongue moved over her midriff leaving wet trails like molten fire while his palms made gentle circles on her nipples until they hardened. Her breasts swelled, and she strained toward the splendid sensation of his touch.

"Tell me what you want," he murmured against her skin.

She pressed his hands firmly against her breasts until they were cupped in his big palms, moved them until they were kneading her yearning flesh. "I want . . . I want your mouth here."

He reached behind her, unhooked her bra, and took it off. Her skin almost ignited when his gaze scorched her breasts. He cupped them in his hands and lifted them, then bent his head to kiss, suck, and bathe them with his tongue.

Never had she felt such an exquisite sensation, yet it was exquisite torment. She wanted more. Her hands stroked his muscular shoulders, his broad back, his thick biceps. "I want to feel your skin against mine," she said, tugging at the red tank top.

He peeled it off and tossed it aside. It landed atop the bedside lamp, muting the light and casting a red glow over the room. He removed his jeans and socks and came to her again with only black silk briefs containing his straining arousal.

Saints above, he was magnificent. She marveled at his well-shaped body, grew fascinated with the triangular patch of hair on his chest. When she threaded her fingers through the dark curls, she was surprised to find them soft. She rubbed her cheek against the downiness and touched a nipple with her tongue. He groaned, and she smiled, reveling in the heady feeling that her touch could affect him so.

He seemed hungry for her, and she was equally hungry for him, to touch, to taste. There wasn't an inch of her that he didn't inflame with his tongue, his lips, his teeth, his fingers.

Stripping away their remaining clothes, he stroked her and kissed her and murmured love words until she writhed with wanting. When she thought she could stand no more, she urged him to her, begged him to fill her emptiness. He left her for a moment to roll on protection, then was back raining kisses along her length.

Kneeling in the juncture of her thighs, he lifted her hips and entered her slowly until he was fully sheathed. She wondered at the marvelous fullness of his fit, the perfect way their bodies meshed.

"*This*," he said, "is where you belong." He drew back, then plunged deeply. "Where you've always belonged."

His words, the sensations, spurred a burst of emotion from her that was so strong, it almost engulfed her. She went wild. He matched her wildness, move for move, in a loving roughness that turned them into two frenzied jungle creatures.

She burned; he fed the flames. She hungered; he filled her, then devoured her. With sweat-slicked bodies, they strove in a primal rhythm to a common goal, urging, demanding, giving, taking, loving. She was in the depths of an active volcano, and she felt the pressure building, building until she was thrust from its core with an explosive convulsion.

She cried out as spasms of ecstasy shook her. He waited a moment, then made two quick thrusts and followed her through the raining fire, his back arched, his deep groan filling the red-tinted room.

"Oh Lorddd," she called out.

After a few moments, he responded, "You took the words out of my mouth." He rolled from atop her and brought her against him. "Woman, you're something else."

She snuggled close and stroked his damp chest. "Something good, or something bad?"

"Good?" He chuckled. "Better than good. I'd say superb, definitely superb. Beyond my wildest dreams. I trust you found it . . . *pleasant*."

She pinched his nipple. He laughed, grabbed her hand, and brought it to his lips. "Does that mean yes?"

"At the risk of inflating your masculine ego, I have to honestly say that I've never experienced anything like it. Do you think it was because I've been celibate for so long?"

He raised up, propped himself on one elbow, and traced her lips with his finger. "I don't know. Why don't we try it again and see."

"But, Shade, you can't—"

"The hell I can't!"

Maggie opened her eyes and tried to stretch, but a large hairy leg lay flung over hers and a tattooed arm held her close against a warm, naked body.

She wiggled a bit and flexed her feet, wincing at the tenderness of her toes and the spot between her legs. She'd heard of people making love all night long, but she'd never *done* it. She had now. Lord, the man was a bull. She sighed. An exquisite bull. Her previous sexual experiences had been amateur bouts; lovemaking with Shade had been The Main Event.

Her stomach growled, and she wiggled again.

Shade kissed her shoulder. "You awake?"

"Uh-huh."

"What are you thinking about?" He turned her to face him.

She smiled. "That I would sell my soul for a warm, fresh bagel and cream cheese."

"Going." He kissed her. "Going." He kissed her again. "Gone." He kissed her a third time, then got up and started dressing.

Gathering the quilt around her, she sat up. "What are you doing?"

"I'm putting on my clothes so I can go get you a fresh bagel."

She laughed. "And where do you expect to find one around here?"

"There's a nice little bakery in Beaumont."

"But that's an *hour's* trip."

"Yep. Why don't you take another little snooze." He sat down beside her to pull on his boots, then dropped a kiss on her nose. "I want to find you right here when I get back."

"But I need to feed Byline."

"That fat rascal can wait another hour. I'll pick up the master key and feed him when I get back. Bye, darlin'."

Maggie had no choice but to stay in his room. Omie Nell didn't come by on Sundays until after lunch, and she didn't want to ask Buck for a key. Not that she was embarrassed to have him know that she'd spent the night with Shade, she told herself. It was simply that she didn't want to fuel Buck's already considerable matchmaking efforts. The idea of Shade and her as a permanent couple was totally outrageous, despite his avowals of love. Pillow talk, nothing more. She'd heard every line in the book.

She pulled the quilt under her chin and tried to go back to sleep, but she felt wide awake and energized. Strange, since she hadn't slept much in bed with Shade. He was a dynamite lover— passionate, considerate, and very, very thorough. Together they'd generated enough electricity to light up Manhattan, Brooklyn, and Queens.

After making love with him, she'd never felt so complete as a woman. He could easily become a habit. No, that kind of thinking was dangerous. As soon as her Tree Hollow story blew the respectable covers of a few weasels, they'd be indicted— or at least be forced to leave in disgrace—and she'd go back to New York where she belonged. She blossomed in the hustle and bustle of the city, and she couldn't imagine Shade fitting into her life there, any more than she would be content to spend the rest of her days cooking turnip greens and listening to grass grow.

Giving up the effort to sleep, she rose, removed the bandages from her feet, which didn't look too bad, and showered. After she toweled off, she put on Shade's robe and rolled the sleeves up a couple of notches. She pulled the lapels up to her face and breathed in the distinctive odor that clung to the fabric.

Barefoot, she padded around the cabin, wondering how to kill the forty-five minutes until his return. She straightened the bed and folded her clothes. Forty-two minutes left. She could—naw, she couldn't do that.

The hell she couldn't.

She made a beeline for the closet.

Inside she found the briefcase still sitting in a back corner behind a duffel bag. She dragged it out, carried it to the bed, and tried to open it.

Locked. Rats!

Hoping to find the key, she rummaged through a box of odds and ends in the top chest drawer. No such luck. Since she didn't have a hairpin, she made do with a fishhook that she straightened with a pair of pliers from his tackle box.

Her lock-picking efforts took nearly twenty minutes and a punctured finger, but she smiled when she heard the telltale click. She wiped her sweaty palms on the robe and released the catches. They sprung open with a loud thunk. Feeling exceedingly guilty, she looked around the room as if she expected to be caught pilfering at any moment. Silly, of course.

Her heart pounding, she slowly opened the lid.

Her eyes widened. She gasped.

"Ohhh . . . my . . . God." The briefcase was full of money.

Neatly banded together were stacks and stacks of twenty- and fifty-dollar bills. There must be thousands and thousands of dollars. She didn't count it. She didn't want to touch it. She slammed the lid down and snapped the clasps.

Holy Moses! How was she going to relock it? She tried using the fishhook, but her hands were shaking so badly that she was afraid she'd scratch the lock or ruin it altogether. Using the tail of the robe, she wiped her fingerprints off the case—why, she didn't know—and returned it to the closet.

Then she paced. She held her head and paced and tried to think of some logical explanation for Shade having that much cash. Bank. Bank. Bank guard. Had he actually said he was a bank guard? No, she'd assumed he was a bank guard.

No, she couldn't be in love with a bank robber.

She froze. *In love?* Where had that come from?

Oh . . . my . . . God. She couldn't be in love with him. Not with a bank robber. Or an embezzler. No, no. He couldn't be an embezzler. But all the alternatives she could think of were as bad or worse. Soldier of fortune. Blackmailer. Drug dealer. Hit man. Hit man? "Ohhh . . . my . . . God."

Maybe he'd won the lottery, she thought hopefully. Get real, she told herself.

Counterfeit. It was counterfeit. Ohhh, Lord.

She dragged the briefcase from the closet again and opened it. She riffled through a band of twenties, but they were all different numbers and out of sequence, and some were more worn than others. The money appeared genuine. She slipped a bill from the middle of the pack and scrutinized it carefully. It looked okay, but what did she know? Should she take a sample to a bank?

No, no, she had to put it back.

She tried to slip the twenty back into the bundle, but it wouldn't go. Her hands shaking, she shoved harder. The paper band broke and twenty-dollar bills flew everywhere.

"Ohhh . . . my . . . God."

Frantically, she gathered up the money and tried to stack it neatly, but her flustered state made neatness impossible. She wrapped the paper band around the bundle, but there was no way she could repair the rip. In desperation, she tucked the broken stack on the bottom, arranged the others to cover it, and stowed the case back in the closet.

She held her head and paced. Shade couldn't be a bank robber, an embezzler, or a drug dealer. Thinking that he was a hit man was ludicrous. And he didn't seem to be the blackmailer type. Could he be part of the mob? Did they have a mob in Texas?

Stop it! As an investigative reporter, she'd been trained not to jump to conclusions before all the facts were collected, but here she was jumping like crazy. Calm down, she told herself. Use your head. Maybe he was involved in something slightly shady, but there could be a perfectly reasonable explanation as well.

All she had to do was ask.

And admit that she'd been snooping. He'd be pissed. He'd be disillusioned.

Maggie had always been a darned good judge of character, and while she couldn't imagine that Shade was a criminal, she knew him well enough to know that he kept his cards close to his vest, so to speak.

Cards. Of course. He was a gambler. It all fit—no regular job, a large sum of cash. No bank account, no records, the IRS would never know. Maybe he was a bookie.

But where was his base of operations? Her eyes narrowed. Was Buck in on this too? Now that she thought of it, this place had a lot of overhead for the small amount of business generated.

For the time being, she'd keep an open mind, her mouth shut, and a sharp eye out.

She considered dressing and leaving before Shade returned, but there was still the matter of the key. And he wouldn't know that she'd seen his stash. In any case, she had no reason to feel afraid of him. He'd always been very gentle and solicitous of her, and not in a million years could she imagine him hurting her. The question was: Could she play it straight and pretend that nothing had happened while he'd been gone?

The question became moot when she heard footsteps on the porch. She scooted across the room, sat down on the small couch, and casually propped her bare feet on the coffee table.

When he came in the door and spotted her, a slow, sexy smile spread over his face, and he bent to kiss her. With the touch of his warm lips on hers, all thoughts of criminality disappeared from her mind.

"I thought you were supposed to stay in bed." She shrugged. "I wasn't sleepy."

He nuzzled her ear. "Mmmm. You smell like my soap. You weren't supposed to get your bandages wet."

"I took them off. My toes are fine."

He tossed the sack he carried on the coffee table, knelt, and examined her feet carefully. "Not too bad. I'll put some more ointment on them." He kissed each instep, then grinned at her. "I'd recommend at least another day of bed rest." He winked. "In my bed. With me."

"I have to work today. My story, remember?"

"When are you going to let me read it?"

She mumbled something noncommittal, then picked up the big bag he'd dropped. "Are these the bagels?"

"Yep. I forgot to ask what kind you liked, so I got a half dozen of everything they had."

"Plain is fine. Or onion. Did you get onion?"

"Yes ma'am, I did. I'll go toast them."

She started to get up. "I'll help."

He restrained her gently. "You stay right there and keep those pretty feet up. Let me take care of you."

"I'm not used to anyone taking care of me."

He kissed her. "It's time you learned. I plan to do a lot of it."

"Oh, you do?" She laughed.

"Yes, love, I do. I have some long-range plans." He nibbled on her ear.

"Paul?"

"Hmmmm?"

"Just Paul. I was trying out the name. Are you going to tell me the rest of it now?"

"Berringer."

"Paul Berringer. Very nice. I like it." Her stomach growled.

He laughed and patted it. "Breakfast is coming up."

As she watched him walk away, she admired his taut derriere, his broad back, his long legs, his easy grace. She sighed. This man couldn't possibly be a criminal. She loved him.

God help her, she loved him.

NINE

Maggie sat at her computer, working on the first draft of her story and keeping one eye on the window. As soon as she saw Shade's pickup leave, she punched the save button and ran for the door. She had no idea how long his errand would take, and she meant to grill Buck within an inch of his life. Three days had passed since she'd found the money, and there hadn't been a single opportunity for her to get Buck alone.

She strolled into the bait shop where Buck was skimming dead minnows from the large container in which they were kept. She peeked over his shoulder. "Seems like a waste."

He shrugged. "Always lose a few. Shade said you was writin' this afternoon."

"I needed to take a break." She ambled to the old-fashioned soft-drink cooler, selected a cola, opened it, then hoisted herself atop the cooler and swung her legs while she sipped from her drink. "I want to ask you a question."

"Ask away."

"Do you know where I might place a bet on a basketball game, a horse race, or something like that?"

"Nope," he said, dumping the dead minnows in a bucket. "Don't know much about that kind of business. I'm not a gamblin' man myself. Sybil don't hold with such as that. There's a race track not too far away. Over the state line in Louisiana. I forget what it's called."

So much for the idea of them running a bookie joint. "Do you think Paul might know?"

"He might, but— Who'd you say?"

She laughed. "I know that Shade's real name is Paul Berringer. He told me. So you don't have to worry about giving away his secrets."

A fisherman came in to buy two dozen night crawlers, so Maggie sat quietly, sipping her drink until the man paid for his worms and left.

"You and Shade are good friends, aren't you?" she asked.

"Yes'um. I reckon he's about the best friend I got. Wouldn't have this place if it wasn't for him."

"Oh? Are you partners in the business?"

"Nope. He wouldn't have none of that. It's mine free and clear."

"You mean he paid for it? Where would he get that kind of money?"

Buck looked at her sharply. "Now, Miss Maggie, I've come to think a lot of you, and I hate to say it, but it appears to me that you've got somethin' up your sleeve besides your arm. I reckon if you've got any more questions, you ought to ask them of Shade. I don't meddle in his business, and he don't meddle in mine."

Maggie inclined her head. "Point taken. Sorry, Buck." She hopped down from the drink cooler and deposited her bottle in the case. "I'd appreciate it if you wouldn't mention our conversation to Shade."

"It ain't my habit to carry tales."

She grinned. "See you later."

Rats! she thought as she trudged back to her cabin. She'd underestimated Buck. And she didn't know much more than when she started. Her deal with Shade to ask one question a day had sort of pooped out. He'd counted the silliest things as serious questions, declared her to be at least ten in the hole, and refused to answer anything of consequence. Of course he'd said it teasingly, but dammit, there were things she wanted to know, needed to know.

She'd demanded that he answer her questions, but he'd only given her that sexy smile that turned her into a babbling idiot, kissed her senseless, and said, "Darlin', the minute you agree to marry me, my life is an open book."

She kept meaning to ferret out an answer or two during an unguarded moment of their love-making—which had been nightly and frequent—but she kept forgetting. Rather, she was always so caught up in passion that she couldn't think. Lord, she adored that scoundrel.

But loving him wasn't enough. And agreeing to marry a man so ill-suited to her lifestyle, and about whose background she had serious doubts, would be the height of lunacy. For all she knew, someone might show up and haul him off to the slammer at any moment.

Rats!

The best thing for her to do would be to finish her story, sell it to the highest bidder in New York, and split. She'd had enough grief in her life.

She returned to her computer and wrote furiously until she heard an insistent knocking. Irritated by the interruption, she got up and stomped to the door, stumbling over Byline on her way.

"Don't you have something better to do?" she asked the cat. "Why don't you go outside and torment Comet?"

"Me-ow."

"I know. His master affects me the same way, only I'm lousy at climbing trees."

When she swung open the door, Shade stood there, a big red-bowed box in his hands. He handed her the box and kissed her cheek.

"What's this?"

He grinned. "Open it and see."

Since the package was wrapped identically to the one he'd given her a few days before, it didn't require a great deal of perspicacity to divine its contents. She ripped off the paper. Boots. Duplicates of her ruined ones.

"Try them on," he said. "I bought a half size longer so you'd have plenty of toe room. And if you wear them a few hours every day, by Saturday, they'll be broken in."

She took off her sneakers and pulled on the boots. She stood and walked around. "Perfect."

He grinned. "I thought they might be. I checked the sizes in your other shoes."

"You sneak!" She whopped his head with the box top.

He laughed, ducked, and pinned her arms. When she opened her mouth to call him a few worse names, his mouth stopped her. The kiss turned steamy. One thing led to another and—well, it was the first time she'd ever made love with her boots on.

❖━━━━━━━━━❖

On Thursday morning, Maggie drove to the nearest pay phone, which was at a service station seven miles away. She didn't want to chance anybody overhearing her conversation with Mel Wanamaker, a free-lance writer and a crusty old character who had been a friend of hers for years. Mel, who'd garnered a couple of Pulitzers along with a lengthy list of other awards, had been around for a long time and knew all the media greats and near-greats in New York.

She laid out her change, took a deep breath, and dialed.

Thank heavens Mel answered.

"Mel? Maggie Marino."

"Where in the hell have you been?"

She laughed. "Hiding from the bad guys."

"Doll, there ain't a hole deep enough. The bad guys outnumber the rest of us at least a hundred to one. When I got back from London, I heard you got canned and had left for parts unknown."

"True. I also got several threatening phone calls, a bullet hole through my window, and a big, black Lincoln tried to use me for paving material. I decided to get out of Dodge City."

"You're pulling my leg, right?"

"Wrong. Mel, I stumbled onto a hot story,

and I do mean hot. I've got the goods on a *major* scandal. The reason I got fired was because my dear old publisher is in the mess right up to his wimpy little bow tie. This one has everything: Sex, drugs, money laundering, every kind of sleaze you can think of." Swearing him to secrecy, she briefly outlined the story and sprinkled in a few names, including the president of one of the city's largest banks, a couple of local politicians, and a mob attorney.

Mel whistled. "Sounds like you're sitting on a keg of dynamite. Can you substantiate this?"

"Yep. I have hours of tapes from several of the kids at Tree Hollow; I have photostatic copies of ledgers; I even have some pictures, very damning pictures. I have boxes of material. I gathered most of the stuff before I left New York. I've done the follow-up on the principals from here."

"Where's here?"

"I'm not telling, Mel. Not even you. Sorry."

She could almost hear his shrug over the phone. "So be it. How did you get hold of the books?"

She laughed. "Now, Mel, you know better than to ask that."

"What are you going to do with it?"

"That's where I was hoping you might help. I'll sell the story to the highest bidder, and I'd like it better if the bid included a permanent job. You know everybody in the business; could you ask around for me, find out who might be interested? You know how to handle it."

He was quiet for a moment. "I'll make a few calls. How do I get in touch with you?"

"I'll phone you on Monday or Tuesday. By then, the piece should be finished." She paused. "Thanks, Mel. Be careful with this. I don't want them coming after you."

"An old warhorse like me? Hell, my hide's too tough."

They said their good-byes, and Maggie hurried back to fix lunch. Mel would have never let her hear the end of it if he'd known where she was and what she was doing.

That evening when Maggie left her cabin to begin dinner, she found Shade sitting outside her door, reared back in his usual pose, his feet propped on the porch rail. Byline was curled in his lap, and Comet lay sleeping by the chair.

"I can't believe that those two aren't fighting," she said. "Did you drug them?"

He laughed. "Nope. They declared a truce on their own. But let's not push it. I'll put Byline inside."

As he closed the door behind the cat, Maggie

noticed a blanket and a large basket by the chair he'd vacated. "What's that?"

"I'm taking you to a very private beach for a picnic."

"A private beach? Where?"

He kissed her nose. "You'll see."

"What about Buck?"

"He's not invited."

"I mean, what about his dinner?"

"While you've been working, I've been frying chicken. I left plenty for him." He tucked the blanket under his arm, picked up the basket, and guided her away from the cabin.

"But this is the way to the river," she said.

"Yep."

"Rivers don't have beaches."

"Trust me."

"Are you sure you know what you're doing?" she asked as he helped her into the small boat.

"Yep."

Using the motor, he ran the flat-bottom upriver for about a mile, then angled for a large sandbar that protruded from the bank and extended a third of the way across the river. Shade got out, pulled the boat aground, then helped Maggie out.

She bent over and scooped a handful of sand and let it sift through her fingers. It was cool, fine, and almost white. "It *is* like a beach."

Grinning, he hoisted the basket and the blanket. "Would I lie to you?"

Instead of answering, she only smiled. *Would he lie? Good question.*

Shade spread the blanket on the soft sandbar, tugged off his battered sneakers, and rolled up his jeans. "Want to look for shells?"

"Seashells? Here? You're kidding."

"Yes. But we can build a sand castle if you'd like."

"You're on." She disposed of her sandals and knelt in an area of damp sand.

For the next half hour, they worked making a lopsided structure, totally unsuited for royalty, except perhaps a frog prince, but they laughed together at their efforts and thoroughly enjoyed their childlike play.

When the turret she'd toiled over collapsed for the third time, Maggie stood and dusted off the seat of her shorts. "That's it," she declared. "Let's eat. Where can I wash my hands?"

"There's a whole river."

"In *that* water with the fish and frogs and snakes? No way." She made a face. "You're teasing again, right?"

"I forget that you're a hothouse flower. Will this do, madame?" He plucked a liter of French bottled water from the basket and presented it as a sommelier would offer a choice wine.

"Well," she replied haughtily, "if you've nothing better, I suppose it will suffice." They grinned at each other as he poured water over her hands, then snapped his handkerchief and extended it with a flourish. After her hands were dry, she examined the fine cotton handkerchief and the discreet monogram in the corner. "P-E-B. What does the E stand for?"

"Ellison."

"Paul Ellison Berringer. Sounds very high-toned. You should be a blue-blooded captain of industry and a member of the country club set with a name like that."

"How about some chicken, mademoiselle?" He held up a drumstick and bowed.

She held out her shorts and curtsied. "Delighted, monsieur." She took the drumstick and nibbled on it while he set out the rest of their fare.

On the sandbar in the Neches River, they dined on chicken, potato salad, and baked beans kept warm in a thermos. They talked of nonsensical things and laughed and ate to the music of rippling water, distant birds, and chirring tree frogs. With her wineglass balanced on her stomach, she lay with her head in his lap, and he fed her grapes as they watched the sun's last rays color the sky in glorious pastels and turn the surface of the river to muted gold.

Sated and totally relaxed, she felt more peaceful than she'd felt in ages, perhaps more than in her whole life.

When the last grape was gone, he slowly traced the lines of her profile, lingering at her mouth to stroke along the sensitive line where her lips met, nudging them apart to slide his finger over the edge of her bottom teeth. Something about the trusting intimacy of the gesture sparked a bittersweet longing deep inside her. So potent was the emotion that tears filled her eyes.

Shade must have noticed, for he said, "Darlin', what's wrong?"

"Nothing is wrong. At this moment everything is very right. This place is like Eden. Life's reality with its malevolence and ugliness seems very far away. I can almost believe that there's no one else in the world but you and me."

"We can stay here forever if you'd like." He outlined her jaw from ear tip to ear tip.

She sighed. "Unfortunately, I have a short attention span. Eden's a nice place to visit, but I wouldn't want to live there. I'd soon get bored with trees and flowers and tranquility. I prefer variety and excitement."

He reached into the basket. "Have an apple," he said, offering one to her.

Maggie laughed and touched the cobra tattoo. "That's my line."

He cocked his eyebrow and said in a slow drawl, "Let's both take a bite and get naked."

Shade tickled her and she giggled, trying to squirm away. He held her fast until she retaliated by tickling his ribs. Clamping his elbows to his sides, he tried to fend off her attempts.

"Aha! Look who's ticklish."

He jumped up and ran—not too fast, she noticed—and she chased him around the sandbar until he allowed her to catch him. Then he scooped her up in his arms and with both of them laughing like carefree children, he whirled her around while she clung to his neck.

She looked up at him, and in the space of two heartbeats, his laughter faded and his expression changed to one of smoldering intensity. "Dear God," he whispered fiercely, "I do love you so."

She cupped his cheek, feeling the faint stubble of beard against her palm, and studied the handsome, rough-hewn face that had turned so fervent, so serious, and marveled that a man like Shade could truly love her. And she believed that he did. How tragic that this idyllic time must end.

No, she didn't want to think about that now. "Kiss me. Make love to me. Here. Now."

Carrying her to the blanket as if she were a precious treasure, he knelt and laid her down gently. As he kissed her and caressed her, they shed their clothes and flung them away into the sand. With the breeze playing over their bodies and twilight creeping across the canopy of evening sky, they made slow, sweet love. Their murmured endearments echoed along the banks of the river and floated downstream with the soft rush of water.

On Friday night, Maggie tested a strand from a large pot of spaghetti. "Needs a few more minutes. How are the meatballs coming?" she asked Shade.

With closed eyes, he inhaled the scent of the bubbling sauce which filled the kitchen with its garlicky, spicy smell, then kissed the tips of his fingers with a loud smack. "Perfection."

Giving a smug bobble of her head, she said, "You know, I think I'm getting the hang of this cooking business. Are you sure Buck likes spaghetti?"

"Darlin', *everybody* likes spaghetti." He hugged her. "You've become a great cook."

"With a lot of help from you. I couldn't have handled it by myself. Have I thanked you lately?"

"Not in the last ten minutes or so."

"Thank you." She draped her arms around his neck and kissed him.

He deepened the kiss, lifted her to the countertop, and stepped between her legs.

"Our dinner is going to ruin if you keep this up," she told him as he rubbed his cheek against her breast.

"Naw. How's the book coming?"

She hesitated. Lord, she hated to keep lying to him. Should she tell him the truth? The facts of her real project almost sprang to her lips, but something made her pause. Not yet.

"My work is coming along fine," she said, hedging.

He rubbed his nose against her cheek. "When are you going to let me read it?"

"Nobody reads my work until it's finished. I'm . . . superstitious."

He chuckled. "You don't strike me as the superstitious type."

"Just goes to show you how little you really know about me."

"I know enough. I know that your favorite color is blue, that you have a tiny mole here," he said, pressing a spot on her left breast, "and that you like being touched here."

Her back arched and she drew in a sharp breath. "I'd better check the spaghetti again."

He chuckled against her ear, then moved away.

Half-dazed, she slid from the counter. Now

what was it that she was supposed to do? Oh, yes, the spaghetti.

"It's done," she declared after testing another strand. "Will you slide the garlic bread under the broiler while I drain this?"

"Your wish is my command."

She laughed. "In my dreams. Is the salad on the table?"

"Yep."

Maggie poured the pasta onto a large platter, then spooned sauce and meatballs on top. "This smells heavenly." She touched a finger to the sauce and tasted it. "You were right about the oregano."

"Would I lie to you?"

She cocked a brow. "Sometimes I wonder." She hoisted the platter and started for the door to the tavern. "I'll take this in," she said over her shoulder, "if you'll get the bread."

When she turned her head back, she spotted a man entering the front door of the tavern. A big, tall man. Wearing a white cowboy hat. With a silver star on his shirt and a gun on his hip. Her heart tripped and blood rushed to her face.

Panicked, she swiftly retreated to the kitchen. "Cheese it! The cops," she hissed to Shade.

"Huh?"

"A Texas Ranger is coming in the front door. Quick, out the back. I'll stall him."

"Maggie—"

"Would you get out of here? Hurry."

"Maggie—"

"Dammit! Move!"

He turned to leave. And not a moment too soon. With both hands in a death grip on the spaghetti platter, she stepped into the doorway just as the Ranger reached the bar.

She pasted a bright smile on her face. "May I help you?"

He tipped his white hat. "Ma'am, I'm looking for a fellow named Paul Berringer. Have you seen him around here?" He moved forward as if to look into the kitchen.

She sidestepped and blocked his way. Fluttering her eyelashes furiously, she drawled, "Why, I don't know. What does this character look like?" He tried to peer around her, but she danced back and forth to obstruct his line of vision.

"He's about my size, green eyes, snake tattoo on his upper arm." He tried peering around her again; she danced around some more.

"Sounds like a desperate character. What's he done?"

"Ma'am, are you trying to hide something? Is somebody in that kitchen?"

She gave him her big-eyed, affronted look. "Why, what a strange notion."

"Ma'am, I'm going to look in that kitchen."

He grasped her lightly by the upper arms and tried to move her aside.

"Like hell you are, buster!"

She wrenched free of his hold and smacked him in the face with the platter of spaghetti. He let out a roar that would have raised the dead.

Shade rounded the corner of the tavern in time to hear Maggie's adversary let out a string of oaths that would have put a lesser woman to blushing. He heard a laugh and a familiar, "Hooweee," from the shadows by the front window.

"Ross," he said, "what in the hell is going on?"

"Hey there, big brother. You're a sight for sore eyes." He slapped Shade on the back, then pointed inside. "I'm watching Holt tangle with a wildcat armed with a plate of spaghetti."

Shade winced as Maggie broke the platter over Holt's head, and Ross laughed as his twin brother slipped on a meatball and busted his keister.

"I think the wildcat's winning," Ross said. "Friend of yours?"

"Your future sister-in-law if I can convince her to marry me."

"No kidding? That's great." He slapped Shade on the back again and pumped his hand. "Think we should go break it up?"

Shade shook his head and stepped away from the window. "Holt won't hurt her, and Maggie can hold her own. Why are the two of you here?"

"Because things are going to hell in a hand basket. Holt and I are Texas Rangers, and damned good ones. We're not cut out to be businessmen. Even if we had the time to run things—which we don't—we don't have the inclination. Mama can't be expected to handle all the family business. We need you, brother."

"What about Jack Rule?" Shade asked, naming the man he'd left in charge.

"Resigned a couple of weeks ago. Left today."

Shade uttered a succinct epithet and turned away.

"People have been antsy about you being gone. The wolves are circling. If you don't come back and tend to things right away, there may not be much left to come back to."

Maggie ran from the kitchen and, out of breath, leaned against a wall. Thank God Buck had come in when he did, and she was able to get away from the Ranger. She'd have to lie low for a while herself. When she heard the soft drone of men's voices from in front of the tavern, she sneaked around the side of the building, pausing in the shadows by the corner so that she could hear.

"How did you find me?" Shade asked.

"Kind of thought you might be here when I talked to Buck the other day. He's a terrible liar, by the way. I checked the license plates of all the cars and trucks around. Found a new pickup registered to you. Just been biding my time." He laughed and Maggie cringed. "A Texas Ranger always gets his man. You coming with us peaceably?"

"I'd rather not," Shade said.

"Don't see any way around it. This is serious business. Sooner or later you have to face the music."

"Give me a couple of days to tie up some loose ends, and I'll go back on my own."

"How do I know that you won't take off for the border and leave us holding the bag?"

Shade laughed, but Maggie thought his laugh sounded hollow. "You have my word on it."

"Fair enough. I'd better go and collect Holt. Hoo-weee, I'll bet he's madder than a flank-strapped bull at a rodeo."

Maggie didn't wait to hear any more. Tears stinging her eyes, she dashed for her cabin. Locking the door behind her, she leaned against it and tried to calm her breathing before she hyperventilated.

She would not go all weepy and hysterical. She would *not*. This was a time for a cool head and cooler analysis.

Despite the fact that she loved him, despite all the rationalizations she'd made to herself about the money in his closet, about his reluctance to discuss his past, she couldn't ignore the truth any longer.

Shade was a wanted man.

Her knees sagged. Dear Lord, what was she going to do?

TEN

If nothing else, she could leave him with his pride intact, Maggie decided as she watched Shade perform on Saturday night. And she *was* leaving. He probably was going to prison, and she was heading back to the real world. She'd finished the story that afternoon. All she had to do was wait until she called Mel on Monday. By next week, she'd be back in the city, on a new job, and riding the crest of her big scoop. She might even win her own Pulitzer for this one.

Of course Shade hadn't admitted that he was going to prison. When he'd come to her door after the Rangers left the night before, he'd innocently asked, "You want to tell me what the hell that was all about?"

His was a good ploy. She'd used the defense/offense reversal often enough to appreciate his technique. She'd shrugged, deciding to play along.

"I don't know what happened. Sometimes when I see a policeman bearing down on me, I go crazy. I guess it was a flashback to my misspent youth. I told you I lived on the streets for a year before I went to live at Tree Hollow."

"But spaghetti in the face?" He laughed. "And why were you trying to warn me away?"

She'd shrugged again, unable to look at him. "He was looking for you. And . . . and when he grabbed me, I acted instinctively."

Shade had grabbed her upper arms and searched her face. "Grabbed you? He didn't hurt you, did he?"

"Not as much as you are now."

Instantly, he'd released his grip. "Sorry," he'd said, hugging her. "I appreciate your concern, but, darlin', nobody wants to haul me off to jail." She'd let it pass. "Buck is cleaning up the mess, and I'm going to go get a couple of pizzas. What do you like on yours?"

The Ranger incident hadn't been mentioned again. They'd eaten pizzas, then retired to her room to make frenzied love most of the night. Shade seemed hesitant to leave her side, but she'd kicked him out Saturday morning and spent the day writing until her piece was as polished as she could make it. And it was damned good if she did say so herself.

The room burst into applause as Shade finished his song. "Thank you," he said in that gravelly voice that she adored. "This is the last appearance I'll be making for a while," he added, and the crowd groaned. He smiled wistfully, and Maggie's heart almost broke. "Tonight, I'd like to sing a new song I wrote for the woman I've asked to be my wife."

She could feel everyone's gaze on her as he began strumming his guitar. When he started singing softly of building sand castles in Eden, her eyes filled with tears, and a roaring in her ears grew so loud that she couldn't hear the rest of the words. Before the song ended, she ran from the room and to the sanctity of her cabin.

She looked down at the new boots she wore, butter-soft and a perfect fit. Yanking off the boots, she threw one across the room. "It's not fair! Dammit, it's not fair!" She threw the other one, and Byline shot under the bed.

An insistent knocking made her stalk to the door and throw it open. Shade leaned against the jamb, his arms crossed, a frown marring his brow.

"Why did you leave?"

"Why did I leave?" she shrieked. "Why did

you announce to the world that you'd asked me to marry you? I've told you a dozen times that I won't."

"Why not?"

"Why not? Why not?" Her voice rose an octave. "Are you crazy? You know why."

"Tell me again."

"Because you're—" She bit back the words she almost said. "Because I don't know anything about you."

"You know enough. You know that you love me."

"That's beside the point," she sputtered. "I don't plan to spend the rest of my life in a god-forsaken dump on a river bottom twenty miles from nowhere. I have my work to think of."

"You're a writer. Writers can write anywhere."

"No, they can't, especially if—" She took a deep breath, then let it out. "I might as well tell you the rest of it. I don't write mysteries. I am—was—an investigative reporter with a large New York daily. I'm free-lancing now."

A thundercloud rolled over his face. "And what are you writing about? Me?"

"No, no, of course not. I'm writing about a scandal in New York. About Tree Hollow. The kids there took me into their confidence and gave me an earful about the criminal abuses going on there. You can't imagine what they've been doing to those kids, the exploitation—"

"What else have you lied to me about?"

"You're a fine one to talk about lying!"

"When have I lied to you?" he roared.

"Lord, deliver me from idiots. Get me back to civilization!"

"Civilization? You think New York is *civilized*? There's a mugging a minute, half the population's on drugs, and people kill each other off faster than rabbits multiply. If you call that cesspool 'civilization,' you're welcome to it."

"You're a fine one to talk!"

"What do you mean by that?"

"With *your* background—or should I say, lack of background?"

"And I suppose a poor, dumb hick like me's not good enough for the hoity-toity reporter from New York City? Well, fine. That's friggin' fine."

He stomped out and slammed the door.

"Damn you, Shade, that's not what I meant," she yelled. But only Byline heard her. She started to go after him, then decided that if there had to be an ending, one way was as good as another. She'd wanted—

Oh, what the hell. They'd both survive.

An engine vroomed to life in the carport next door and gravel spewed as Shade's truck roared away. It was just as well, she told herself.

But she threw herself across the patchwork quilt on her bed and wept.

Maggie awoke Sunday morning with her eyes grainy, her clothes wrinkled, and wrapped in the quilt. Her first thought was of Shade. She jumped up and ran outside.

His pickup was nowhere in sight.

She trudged back inside and flopped onto the bed. Byline hopped up beside her and walked over her stomach. She stroked his back and stared at the ceiling. "I guess it's just you and me, guy."

"Meow." He rubbed his head under her chin.

"Thanks."

A few minutes later, she forced herself to get up and shower. By rote, she fed the cat, fixed a mug of coffee, and dressed. But it was Sunday, and she had nothing to do. She didn't have to cook; her story was finished; Shade was gone.

One thing was certain: She couldn't stay alone in the cabin all day. She'd go bonkers. She grabbed her keys and her bag and drove to Beaumont. At a little restaurant she found interesting, she had brunch and read a couple of newspapers while lingering over a second, then a third cup of coffee. When the lunch crowd began arriving, she vacated her table, went to the mall, and wandered through the shops.

Soon bored, she visited several of the town's many museums, but none held her interest. She'd never felt so alone in her life.

She found a small park and sat on the grass, watching families and children laugh and play together while her sense of separateness and misery increased. Unable to tolerate it any longer, she left and simply drove around until she found herself back at Hebert's Restaurant. She thought of a good novel, but the bookstore was closed, so she went into Hebert's for an early dinner. At least she felt a semblance of familiarity there.

After dinner, she sat through two movies, neither of which excited her very much, then drove back to her cabin. The carport of number three was still empty, and no light filtered through the cabin's front window.

She had a murderous headache.

Monday morning began no better than Sunday. Maggie walked to the bait shop, seeking a friendly face. She found Buck stocking the bait cooler with cups of worms.

"Mornin'," he said, smiling broadly.

"Good morning. You look very happy today."

"Yep. Sybil called a while ago. She's gonna be home day after tomorrow."

"I'll bet you're pleased about that."

He grinned. "Shore am."

She was determined not to ask, but the words popped out of her mouth in spite of her resolve. "Have you heard from Shade?"

Buck sobered. "Called yesterday. Told me to hold on to his stuff." He turned back to stocking the cooler.

Her chest felt as if a steel band were constricting it. "Where did he call from?"

"Didn't ask."

"I see." She pressed her hand to her breast and took a deep breath. "Speaking of calls, I need to make a couple. I'm going to use the pay phone next door."

"Hep yourself."

Maggie walked into the tavern where this chapter of her life had all begun. She strolled over to the pool table and ran her fingers over the smooth green felt and remembered Shade bending over it, cue stick in hand. Had it truly been less than three weeks ago? It seemed like a lifetime.

She nudged the three ball and watched it roll down the table, then turned away. The place with its familiar smell of pine cleaner and stale tobacco and its dance floor and bandstand seemed large and very empty. She could close her eyes and almost hear the band playing, Shade singing, and cries of "yeee-haa" echoing from the walls.

She shook her head and pulled a handful of coins from her pocket.

Her first call, to Mel, produced only a busy signal. The second, to her uncle's attorney, accomplished better results. Someone had made an offer on Silas's river property, and Maggie was pleasantly surprised by the amount. She'd had no idea it was worth that much or that the deal could be concluded so quickly.

"The real estate agent called me not fifteen minutes ago," the attorney said. "If you accept the offer, and it sounds like more than a fair price to me, we can have the papers drawn up and your money in the bank by the end of the week."

"Tell the agent that I accept."

After she hung up, she tried Mel again. This time he answered.

"Mel, Maggie. I called you earlier, but your line was busy."

He sighed. "I was making one last effort to sell your story."

Her stomach turned over, and she felt the

blood drain from her face. "One last effort? That doesn't sound good."

"Sweetheart, it's bad. Somebody has put the word out about you, and I'd guess that it's Robert Bartlett and his cronies. Your ex-publisher is a powerful man. You're a pariah in this town, doll. The story is that you're unstable, that you cracked up, and when your paper had to fire you for your bizarre behavior, you attacked Bartlett and vowed to ruin him. They say you falsified stuff. None of your reporting's reliable."

"But Mel, that's not true."

"You know it, and I know it, but nobody will take a chance on getting sued publishing anything that comes from you. Even if you got an editor on your side, your story wouldn't see print."

She leaned her back against the wall to keep from falling. "What am I going to do?"

"You could always make a nice piece of change from the grocery store tabloids."

"I'd never sink that low. My credibility would be shot for sure. Everybody knows that most of the swill they print is lies."

"I'm sorry, Maggie. I did the best I could."

"I know you did, Mel. Thanks."

Still stunned when she hung up, Maggie slid slowly down the wall and sat on the floor, her knees drawn to her chest.

◆━━━━━━━━━◆

Paul Berringer sat at his hand-carved desk in his penthouse office, trying to unsnarl the mess that he'd found on his return. He'd spent the entire day Sunday working, and he'd been in his office since dawn.

He picked up a gold pen to sign a stack of correspondence, but his hand wouldn't obey him. He cursed, threw the pen across the room, and wheeled his chair around to stare out the window.

He was miserable, damned miserable. But the reasons for his misery were different from those he'd felt when he'd been in this same spot a few months ago.

Or were they?

Thinking he was in the throes of a mid-life crisis, he'd dropped out and gone off chasing rainbows, imagining that he'd be happy fulfilling the fantasies of his youth. That hadn't been the answer. Oh, he enjoyed singing and writing songs, but a musician's life wasn't for him. He hadn't been happy until he'd found Maggie.

Maggie. How she consumed his thoughts.

His love for her had filled all the empty places in his soul. Now . . .

Damn! What a fool he'd been, storming off like a belligerent adolescent, irate that Maggie had lied to him and furious that she couldn't accept him as he was. But hadn't his lie been worse? A lie of omission, granted, but a lie nonetheless. He'd been unfair to her in not telling her the truth about himself. He'd always wanted someone who loved him for the person he was, not someone who saw dollar signs when she looked at him. But in fact he *was* wealthy. He wasn't a shiftless river-bottom bum, and that's what he was asking Maggie to commit to.

Maggie was the sunshine in his life, his destiny, his other half. Was he going to let senseless pride destroy his chance to have the woman he loved by his side?

Hell, no.

Lunch was an unpleasant affair. Oh, the food was edible, or what she tasted was, but she and Buck felt uncomfortable without Shade there. She told Buck that she would move out the following day and stay at a motel in town until Silas's property was sold. He tried, in his endearingly awkward way, to make her feel welcome to stay, but she declined.

After the noon dishes were washed, Maggie went to her cabin and packed most of her things. She even loaded her computer, her printer, and the boxes of Tree Hollow research into the station wagon.

Restless, filled with overwhelming sadness, she strolled down the tree-lined path to the river. The pines sighed overhead, and the oak leaves fluttered in the breeze and whispered with an empathetic melancholy. Even the birds seemed to have selected sorrowful songs.

She sat on the sandy bank near the pier and watched the silt-clouded water flow by in its relentless journey to the Gulf. Life went on. And on.

Being maligned and unable to sell her story had been a blow, a tough one. But somehow she would recover. She was a fighter, a survivor, and she'd survived worse disasters. But the most devastating blow was losing Shade.

She couldn't think of a single time in her entire thirty-five years that she had ever been so gloriously happy as she had been with him. Why had she thrown it away without a fight? Giving up was alien to her nature.

If they had talked, really talked, instead of butting stubborn, prideful heads, they could have found a solution to all their problems. After discovering the money in his cabin and agonizing over the visits from the Texas Ranger, she'd assumed the worst. She couldn't imagine the Shade that she knew doing anything illegal. And if he'd had a brush with the law . . . well, they could work it out.

Shade was enormously talented, talented enough to succeed as a songwriter or performer if she encouraged him. Maybe they could go to Nashville. She could find a job on a paper there, and with the money from her river property, they could make it until he broke into the business.

But Shade was gone. Driven away by her idiocy. By her misguided sense of what was important. By her failure to love him unconditionally.

But she did love him with all her heart, no matter who he was or what he'd done. If she could only tell him.

Drawing her knees to her chest and leaning her forehead on them, she wept, great racking sobs.

When Shade saw Maggie sitting on the sandy bank crying, a knife slashed through his gut. "Darlin', what's wrong?"

She looked up at him, tears filling her marvelous eyes and trailing over her lovely face. "Shade?"

Unconcerned with his dress slacks, he knelt beside her and gathered her into his arms. "Oh, love, don't cry. Tell me what's wrong, and I'll make it right. I thought that by now you'd have a dozen offers on your story and be ecstatic."

She shook her head and tried to stop the tears, but they kept coming until the shoulder of his shirt was drenched. "I've been blacklisted. Nobody will buy my story."

"Those sons of bitches! How dare they upset you like this. I'll—"

"That's not why I'm crying."

"It isn't?"

She shook her head against his shoulder. "That was bad, but—but losing you was worse."

"It was?"

"I love you so much." She sobbed into his shirtfront.

"Enough to marry me?"

Her smile melted his heart. "I'll marry you tomorrow," she said. "Today, if you want. We can work things out."

She told him her incredible idea of moving to Nashville, and he smiled, delighting in her offer to support him until he could break into the country-music business.

He kissed her to shut her up. But his love, his hunger quickly turned to passion, and they made glorious love on the riverbank with his shirt and hers spread beneath her.

Afterward, they lay sated in the dappled sunlight with her snuggled close the way he liked.

"Shade?"

"Hmmm?"

"Don't you think we'd better get dressed? What if a fisherman comes along?"

He laughed. "He'd get an eyeful, wouldn't he? But you're right." He stood, pulled her to her feet, and kissed her nose. "I don't always have good sense when I'm with you." While they dressed, he said, "Honey, I'm sorry about your story. Tell me what happened."

As she related the situation, an anger built in him like nothing he'd ever experienced before. He cursed, loudly, then started up the trail at a fast clip, pulling Maggie along.

"Shade! Slow down. Why are you so upset?"

"Sorry, darlin'." He hugged her to his side and continued more slowly. "I'm just furious with those bastards for giving you grief." When they arrived at her door, he said, "Pack a bag. Casual clothes and a couple of nice outfits. Can you be ready in half an hour?"

"Yes, but where are we going?"

He smiled. "You'll see."

Maggie was ready in twenty minutes, which was a good thing because Shade was knocking on the door. She opened it and gasped. He stood there looking like a million bucks in his Armani suit and a silk tie.

"Your clothes!"

He grinned. "The others were a little worse for wear. You ready?"

She nodded. "What about Byline? I can't go off and leave him."

"I've already talked to Buck. He'll feed the cat." He picked up her suitcase. "Bring a copy of your story."

"Why?"

"I want to read it."

"Okay." She shrugged and located her satchel and her handbag. When he guided her outside, she gasped again. A sleek, low-slung Ferrari sat outside her door like a big black pile of money. "Whose is this?"

"Mine."

"It must have been a *big* heist."

"Pardon?"

"Never mind."

There had to be a logical explanation, she kept telling herself as they headed northwest. But she wouldn't ask about the car, about the money. The threat of lashes from a cat-o'-nine-tails wouldn't make her ask. Sooner or later he would explain. She could be patient.

She roused when the car stopped. "I must have dozed off. Where are we?"

"Crockett."

"As in Davy?"

"Yep. We need gas."

Checking her watch, she was surprised to find that she'd slept so long. She went to the ladies' room and washed her face. Half a dozen men were gathered around and admiring the car when she came out.

"It is a beautiful machine," she said to Shade. "I'll bet it drives like a dream."

"Want to try it?"

She hesitated, but he urged her, saying that he'd like to read her story while she drove. She got behind the wheel and, with a few instructions, was off like a shot. After a few miles, she began to understand why men loved Ferraris . . . and Porsches. It was power, control.

They stopped for coffee and Shade brought her story with him, finishing the last few pages as they waited for their order. She watched as he turned over the last page, then gathered and tapped the edges of the papers into a neat stack.

"Well?" she asked.

"Maggie . . ." he said, then paused as if trying to think of the proper words. "It's brilliant. I never dreamed that you were such a gifted writer."

She glowed. "Thank you. I think it's the best work I've ever done."

"Are all your facts substantiated?"

"Every single one."

"This has to be published," he said, his finger

stabbing the pages for emphasis. "The director of Tree Hollow and its board ought to be castrated with dull hedge clippers and thrown into solitary confinement for the rest of their lives."

"I'd settle for tar, feathers, and a rail out of town."

He laughed. "You're more generous than I am. Drink up. We have places to go and things to do."

He drove the rest of the way to Dallas at a speed considerably over the limit. It was dark when they entered a winding drive and stopped in front of a well-lighted building that looked like a posh California country club.

"Where are we?" Maggie asked.

"Home."

"*Whose* home?"

"Mine. And yours if you like it. If not, we'll build another one."

"Holy Moses," she said as he ushered her into a foyer larger than her whole condo. Her eyes grew bigger and bigger as he led her to a huge living area that could have been a centerfold for *House Beautiful.*

"I take it that you like it?"

"What's not to like? It's stunning. What did you say you did for a living? Insurance?"

"A company."

"Real estate?"

"Our family has quite a bit of it, mostly high-rise office buildings."

"And banks," she said. "Did you mention banks? A guard or something like that was the impression you gave me."

He cleared his throat. "I recall that I said I kind of looked after things. And I do. Our family is a major stockholder, and I'm chairman of the board." He watched her closely, obviously anticipating her reaction.

She tried to keep a straight face, to look stern even, but laughter exploded from her. "I thought you might be a bank *robber*."

He started laughing, and they fell into each other's arms. He hugged her and kissed her. "Sure you don't mind all this?"

"Are you kidding? This is like a fairy tale. It sure beats the franks and beans I thought we were going to have to live on when I was going to support us in Nashville."

"Darlin', franks and beans would be a king's feast if I shared them with you." He rubbed his nose against hers. "Want dinner now or later?"

"Later. I want to see the rest of this fabulous house."

"Would you mind showing yourself around for a couple of minutes? I need to make a few phone calls in my study. Explore every nook and cranny to your heart's content. We're alone. There's a swimming pool downstairs."

"In the *basement*?"

"Yep. I'll meet you there after a while."

Maggie did explore everywhere, peeking into the pantry of a kitchen to die for, running her finger along the polished cherry surface of a dining room table that could easily seat twelve, and testing a bed in one of six magnificently decorated bedrooms. There was a morning room, a sun room, a game room, and a couple of rooms that she wasn't sure how to label. She didn't venture into what she assumed was his study.

Downstairs, she found a complete gym, a sauna, and the pool, softly lit with interior lighting. It looked so inviting that she couldn't resist. She pulled off her sandals and dipped a toe in the water. Perfect.

She looked around, wondering if there were bathing suits available. Then she grinned. What the heck. She pulled off her clothes, laid them on a chair, and dived in.

"Like Venus rising from the sea," Shade said as she surfaced.

She laughed. "Hardly. How about Maggie rising from a chlorinated pool?"

"Even better. Mind if I join you?"

"Please do."

He stripped and slid into the water behind

her. He kissed her shoulder and nibbled her ear. "Did you explore?"

"Hmmm. Everything is beautiful."

"Then you'd like to live here? With me?"

"Yep." She turned in his arms and kissed him. They promptly sank. They rose, laughing and sputtering.

"I think we'd better move to the shallow end."

They stroked to chest-deep water and came together again to embrace. "You're a real Texas millionaire, aren't you?"

"Yep."

"You have pots and pots of money?"

"Pots and pots. Does that make you love me more?"

"Nope."

"Less?"

"Nope."

"Dear heaven, woman, I love you."

His mouth covered hers with a kiss so sizzling that she wouldn't have been surprised to see steam rising from the water. He pulled away and her mouth followed his, straining to recapture it.

"We have to talk about some things now, before I forget and lose myself entirely in you."

"What things?"

"First, after we're married, are you still going to want to work?"

"Of course. I love writing, and country club teas bore me. Do you mind?"

"Not if it makes you happy. We have a couple of good newspapers around that would be damned glad to have you. Second, if you could name the two most prestigious news magazines in the United States, which two would you name?"

Puzzled by the bizarre question, she nevertheless answered. He nodded.

"If you could have your Tree Hollow article showcased in one of them, which would it be?"

"Oh, come on, Shade. That's a pipe dream."

"Name one."

She did, and he grinned. "They're both offering you big bucks for the story."

Maggie squealed. "You're kidding?"

"Nope. I just talked to the publishers of both of them."

She hugged him and rained kisses all over his face. "You're wonderful. How did you manage it?"

He grinned and held up his face for more kisses. "I may tell you on our fiftieth anniversary. And speaking of anniversaries, we need to plan our wedding. What do you think about here, next Saturday? My mother could make it anytime, but I'd like for my brothers to be here."

"Saturday is fine. I'm eager to meet your mother and your brothers."

"The twins? You've already met them."

She frowned. "I have?"

"Uh-huh." He chuckled. "They're Texas Rangers."

A vision came of a tall man in a black hat and another equally tall one in a white hat . . . and—

"Ohhhh . . . my . . . Lord . . . the spaghetti."

Shade laughed and kissed her with all the love that was in him.

EPILOGUE

The minister, who stood in front of a bank of white roses and lush greenery, smiled. "You may kiss the bride."

Shade lifted the short veil and kissed the woman he loved more than life itself. And she kissed him back just as fervently.

"Hooo-wee, big brother, don't eat her up."

Susan Sinclair Berringer poked her husband in the ribs. "Hush, Ross, you'll embarrass her."

"Oh, darlin'," he said, kissing his own wife. "I was only funnin'. Besides, I don't think Maggie embarrasses easily."

"That's the truth," Holt whispered to his twin. "And she packs one hell of a wallop with a dish of spaghetti."

Cory, Holt's very pregnant wife laughed. "I wish I could have seen that."

Holt cleared his throat. "Ruined my damned hat."

Eleanor Berringer hushed her grown sons, and like chastised children, their faces sobered and their posture straightened.

When the glowing couple turned to face the small gathering, Eleanor stepped forward with the help of her cane to embrace her new daughter-in-law. The tall, white-haired woman's strong face softened with a smile that lit eyes almost the same pale green hue as her eldest son's. "Welcome to our family," she said.

Family. The word warmed Maggie. "I'm very happy to be a part of it."

"I get to kiss the bride next," Ross said, moving toward her.

Holt cut him off. "The hell you do. I'm next."

Buck Faulkner stepped in front of both of them. "I believe the honor is mine."

Maggie laughed and offered her cheek to the dear man in the ill-fitting suit. He kissed her and introduced her to Sybil, a tiny woman with soft brown eyes.

While Holt and Ross jostled and joked, Cory stepped forward and took Maggie's hands in hers. "We're so happy for you and Paul. I think you're perfect for him."

Maggie beamed at her new sister-in-law. "Thanks. I think so too. When's the baby due?"

"Babies," Cory said. "I'm having twins in about two weeks."

"Me too," whispered Susan.

Maggie lifted her eyebrows.

Susan laughed. "Not in two weeks. More like seven months. I just found out."

Maggie hugged her. "That's wonderful. Are you going to keep the bookstore?"

"Of course. All the Berringer women are independent types. Cory still runs her perfumery."

Maggie sniffed her wrist. "I love the scent you made for me. Is it a special blend?"

Cory smiled. "It's called Nightshade."

Maggie laughed. "Very appropriate."

Eleanor said, "I understand that additional congratulations are in order for you, Maggie. Paul tells me that you're going to work for the *Dallas Morning News.*"

"As soon as we return from our honeymoon. I'm very excited about it."

The twins approached. "We've decided," Ross said. "I get the first kiss. Holt gets the first dance."

Shade elbowed his brothers aside. "Uh-uh. I want to kiss my bride again, and the first dance is mine." He kissed Maggie, nodded to the band, and pulled her onto the dance floor with him.

"Have I told you lately how much I love you?" he asked.

"Uh-huh, but tell me again."

"Mrs. Berringer, I love you."

"And I love you."

As the band played, he held her close and sang softly of building sand castles in Eden.

In the corner, Byline and Comet curled next to each other and went to sleep.

Maggie's Lemon-Basil Mushroom Soup

1 ¼ cups chopped onions
1 cup chopped celery
4 garlic cloves, minced

1 pound sliced fresh
 mushrooms
1 cup sliced carrots
¼ cup margarine

Sauté the above ingredients in margarine until tender and combine with the following in a large stockpot:

6 cups water
½ cup chopped fresh basil*
1 teaspoon pepper
½ cup wild rice (rinsed)

1 10¾-oz. can un-
 diluted cream of
 chicken soup
3 14½-oz. cans chicken
 broth
1 teaspoon lemon juice
¼ cup long grain white
 rice

Bring the ingredients to a boil, then reduce heat. Cover and simmer until rice is tender, approximately 30 minutes. Garnish individual servings with thin lemon slices and grated Parmesan cheese. Makes 16 one-cup servings.

---

*As a substitute for fresh basil, 1 tablespoon dry basil plus ½ cup fresh or frozen chopped spinach may be used.

Maggie's Carrots Grand Marnier

2 pounds fresh carrots,
  peeled and cut into
  ½-inch slices
½ teaspoon salt
¼ cup butter or
  margarine

1 cup white sugar
1 12 oz. jar orange
  marmalade
¾ cup Grand Marnier
  liqueur
Approximately ¼
  teaspoon nutmeg

Combine carrots and salt in saucepan with water to cover. Cover and cook over medium heat until slightly tender (about 15 minutes for fresh carrots, longer for packaged ones). Drain and set aside.

Melt butter or margarine in a large heavy skillet. Add sugar, marmalade, and ½ cup of the Grand Marnier. Stir over low heat until ingredients are well dissolved and bubbly. Add carrots and simmer uncovered for about 30 minutes or until carrots are shiny and candied. Add remaining Grand Marnier. Sprinkle nutmeg over top before serving. May be made ahead and reheated. Serves 6 to 8.

Shade's Chicken and Dumplings

1 4- to 5-pound fat
  hen or roasting
  chicken (a fryer or
  selected chicken
  parts may be sub-
  stituted in a pinch)
1 rib celery

¼ medium onion
½ teaspoon dried parsley
2 teaspoons salt
Black pepper to taste

Put cut-up chicken in a large pot and cover with approximately 8–10 cups cold water. Add remaining ingredients and bring to a boil. Every once in a while, you'll have to skim foam that forms on the broth. Reduce heat and simmer until tender, about 2 hours or more. Remove chicken and vegetables from broth. Strip chicken from bones and reserve to add a portion to dumplings as desired. Reserve about 2½ quarts broth for dumplings. Extend with water if necessary or add canned broth if more liquid is needed at any point during preparation.

Dumplings

⅓ cup shortening
⅔ cup water
  (or chicken broth)
1 teaspoon salt
1½ to 2 cups all-purpose flour
Black pepper to taste
¼ cup milk

Combine shortening, water, and salt in a large mixing bowl. Slowly add flour, mashing and stirring with a fork until a paste is formed, then continue to add flour until mixture is the consistency of biscuit dough. Divide into 2 balls and roll each on a *well*-floured pastry board until piecrust thin. Cut into strips about 1 inch by 3 to 4 inches. Drop strips, one at a time, into gently boiling broth (a rolling boil, not a vigorous one or you'll have a mess all over the stove), pushing down as needed. Cover, cook on low heat for 20 minutes. Uncover and simmer for an additional 5 minutes, adding ¼ cup milk. Add chicken. Turn off heat and let rest for 20 minutes before serving. Serves 6 to 8 normal people, 3 to 4 *big* eaters.

(These are not Pennsylvania-puffy dumplings. These are East Texas, stick-to-your-ribs dumplings that cook up thin and with some substance. They take up most of the liquid and sit on your stomach like matzo balls.)

Shade's Corn Bread

1 ⅓ cups yellow cornmeal
½ cup flour
1 teaspoon salt
½ teaspoon baking soda
2 heaping tablespoons baking powder
3 tablespoons oil
1 egg, beaten

1 cup buttermilk
½ + cup water (depends on consistency of buttermilk)
Yankees may want to add 1 or 2 tablespoons of sugar

Preheat oven to 450°. Heat 2 tablespoons of the oil in a well-seasoned 10-inch iron skillet and keep warm while mixing ingredients. (If no seasoned iron skillet is available, use an equivalently sized heavy baking pan, sprayed with vegetable oil and not heated.)

In a large bowl, combine dry ingredients and mix well. Beat buttermilk, remaining oil, and egg and add to dry mixture with a few swift strokes. Mixture should be the consistency of cake batter. If too thick, add a small amount of water. Make sure skillet is very hot—but don't set the kitchen on fire. Pour batter into sizzling skillet and bake at 450° about 20 to 25 minutes until top is lightly browned. Turn onto plate. Serve warm with butter to use as a pusher for black-eyed peas, purple-hulled peas, pinto beans, or to sop pot likker from turnip greens.

THE EDITOR'S CORNER

Discover heavenly delights and wicked pleasures with **ANGELS AND OUTLAWS**! In the six terrific books in next month's lineup, you'll thrill to heroes who are saints and sinners, saviors and seducers. Each one of them is the answer to a woman's prayer . . . and the fulfillment of dangerous desire. Give in to the sweet temptation of **ANGELS AND OUTLAWS**—you'll have a devil of a good time!

Sandra Chastain starts things off in a big way with **GABRIEL'S OUTLAW**, LOVESWEPT #672. When he's assigned to ride shotgun and protect a pouch of gold en route to the capitol building during Georgia's Gold Rush Days, Gabriel St. Clair tries to get out of it! He'd be sharing the trip, and *very* close quarters, with Jessie James, the spitfire saloon singer whose family has been feuding with his for years . . . and whose smoky kisses had burned him long ago. Gabe had been her first love, but Jessie lost more than her heart when Gabe left the mountain. Seeing him again awakens wicked longings, and Jessie responds with abandon to the man who has always known how to drive her wild. Sandra combines humor and passion to make **GABRIEL'S OUTLAW** a sure winner.

In **MORE THAN A MISTRESS**, LOVESWEPT #673, Leanne Banks tells the irresistible story of another member of the fascinating Pendleton family. You may remember Carly Pendleton from **THE FAIREST OF THEM ALL**, and Garth Pendleton from **DANCE WITH THE DEVIL**. This time we meet Daniel, a man who is tired of being the dependable big brother, the upstanding citizen, and only wants the woman who has haunted his dreams with visions of passion that he's never known. Determined to hide her slightly shady past, Sara Kingston resists Daniel's invitations, but his gaze warms her everywhere he looks. Fascinated by the recklessness beneath his good-guy smile, she yields to temptation—and finds herself possessed. Look forward to seeing more stories about the Pendleton brothers from Leanne in the future.

Marcia Evanick delivers her own unique outlaw in **MY SPECIAL ANGEL**, LOVESWEPT #674. Owen Prescott thinks he's dreaming as he admires the breathtaking beauty on the huge black horse who arrives just in time to save his neck! Nadia Kandratavich is no fantasy, but a sultry enchantress who brought her entire family of Gypsies to live on her ranch. Nadia knows she has no business yearning for the town's golden boy, but his kisses make her hot, wild, and hungry. When prophecy hints that loving this handsome stranger might cost her what she treasures most, Nadia tries to send him away. Can he make her understand that her secrets don't matter, that a future with his Gypsy princess is all he'll ever want? Shimmering with heartfelt emotion, **MY SPECIAL ANGEL** is Marcia at her finest.

BLACK SATIN, LOVESWEPT #675 is from one of our newest stars, Donna Kauffman. A dark bar might be the right place for Kira Douglass to hire an outlaw, but Cole Sinclair isn't looking for a job—and figures the lady with the diamond eyes needs a lesson in playing with danger. He never thought he'd be anyone's hero, but somehow she breathes life back into his embittered soul. She's offered him anything to recover her stolen dolphin; now she vows to fight his demons, to prove to him that she loves him, scars and all, and always will. Donna works her special magic in this highly sensual romance.

Our next outlaw comes from the talented Ruth Owen in **THE LAST AMERICAN HERO**, LOVESWEPT #676. Luke Tyrell knows trouble when he sees it, but when Sarah Gallagher begs the rugged loner to take the job on her ranch, something stirs inside him and makes him accept. His gaze makes her feel naked, exposed, and shamelessly alive for the first time in her life, but can she ignite the flames she sees burning in this sexy renegade's eyes? Branding her body with his lips, Luke confesses his hunger—but hides his fear. Now Sarah has to show him that the only home she wants is in his arms. Fast-rising star Ruth Owen will warm your heart with this touching love story.

Rounding out this month's lineup is **BODY AND SOUL**, LOVESWEPT #677 by Linda Warren. Though Zeke North acts as if the smoky nightclub is the last place on earth he wants to be, he's really imagining how it would feel to make love to a woman whose hands create such sensual pleasure! Chelsea Connors is a seductive angel whose piano playing could drive a man mad with yearning, but he doesn't want to involve her in his brother's trouble. Her spirit is eager for the music she and Zeke can make together. Chelsea aches to share his fight and to soothe old sorrows. He's never taken anything from anyone before for fear of losing his soul, but Chelsea is determined to hold him by giving a love so deep he'd have no choice but to take it. Linda delivers a sexy romance that burns white-hot with desire.

Happy reading!

With warmest wishes,

Nita Taublib

Nita Taublib

Associate Publisher

P.S. Don't miss the spectacular women's novels coming from Bantam in March: **SILK AND STONE** is the spellbinding, unforgettably romantic new novel from nationally bestselling author Deborah Smith; **LADY DANGEROUS** by highly acclaimed Suzanne Robinson pits two powerful characters against each other for a compelling, wonderfully entertaining romance set in Victorian England; and finally, **SINS OF INNOCENCE** by Jean Stone is a poignant novel of four women with only one thing in common: each gave her baby to a stranger. We'll be giving you a sneak peek at these terrific books in next month's LOVESWEPTs. And immediately following this page, look for a preview of the spectacular women's fiction books from Bantam *available now!*

Don't miss these exciting books by your favorite Bantam authors

On sale in January:

THE BELOVED SCOUNDREL
by Iris Johansen

VIXEN
by Jane Feather

ONE FINE DAY
by Theresa Weir

Nationally bestselling author of
THE MAGNIFICENT ROGUE
and
THE TIGER PRINCE

Winner of *Romantic Times*
"Career Achievement" award

Iris Johansen

THE BELOVED SCOUNDREL

Marianna Sanders realized she could not trust this dark and savagely seductive stranger who had come to spirit her away across the sea. She possessed a secret that could topple an empire, a secret that Jordan Draken was determined to wrest from her. In the eyes of the world the arrogant Duke of Cambaron was her guardian, but they both knew she was to be a prisoner in his sinister plot—and a slave to his exquisite pleasure . . .

"Take off your cloak," he repeated softly as his fingers undid the button at her throat. She shivered as his thumb brushed the sensitive cord of her neck.

"It's not a barrier that can't be overcome." He slid the cloak off her shoulders and threw it on the wing chair by the fire. His gaze moved over the riding habit that was as loose and childlike as the rest of the clothes in her wardrobe. "And neither is that detestable garment. It's merely annoying."

"I intend to be as annoying as possible until you give Alex back to me." She added in exasperation, "This is all nonsense. I don't know what you hope to gain by bringing me here."

"I hope to persuade you to be sensible."

"What you deem sensible. You haven't been able to accomplish that in the last three years."

"Because Gregor took pity on you, and I found his pity a dreadful contagious disease." He stepped forward and untied the ribbon that bound one of her braids. "But I'm over it now. Patience and the milk of human kindness are obviously of no avail. I can't do any worse than I—Stand still. I've always hated these braids." He untied the other braid. "That's better." His fingers combed through her hair. "Much better. I don't want to see it braided again while we're here."

The act was blatantly intimate, and her loosened hair felt heavy and sensual as it lay against her back. He was not touching her with anything but his hands in her hair, but she could feel the heat of his body and smell the familiar scent of leather and clean linen that always clung to him. With every breath she drew she had the odd sensation that he was entering her, pervading her. She hurriedly took a step back and asked, "Where am I to sleep?"

He smiled. "Wherever you wish to sleep." A burgundy-rich sensuality colored his voice.

"Then I wish to sleep in Dorothy's house in Dorchester."

He shook his head. "Not possible." He indicated the staircase. "There are four bedchambers. Choose which one you like. I usually occupy the one at the end of the hall."

She stared at him uncertainly.

"Did you think I was going to force you? I'm sorry to rob you of your first battle, but I have no taste for rape. I'm only furnishing a setting where we'll be close, very close. I'll let Fate and Nature do the rest." He nodded to a door leading off the parlor. "Your workroom. I've furnished it with tools and glass and paint."

"So that I can make you a Window to Heaven?" She smiled scornfully. "What are you going to do? Stand over me with a whip?"

"Whips aren't the thing either. I wanted you to have something to amuse you. I knew you were accustomed to working, and I thought it would please you."

She crossed the parlor and threw open the door to reveal a low-ceilinged room with exposed oak beams. She assumed the dark green velvet drapes covered a window. The room was not at all like her workroom in the tower.

But a long table occupied the center of the room and on that table were glass and tools and paints.

Relief soared through her, alleviating a little of the tension that had plagued her since they had left Cambaron.

Salvation. She could work.

"And you, in turn, will amuse me." He gestured to the large, thronelike high-backed chair in the far corner. "I know you were reluctant three years ago to let me watch you at your craft, but circumstances have changed."

"Nothing has changed." She strode over to the

window and jerked back the curtains to let light pour into the room, then went to the table and examined the tools. "I'll ignore you now, as I would have then."

"You wouldn't have ignored me," he said softly. "If I hadn't been a soft fool, you would have been in my bed before a week had passed. Perhaps that very night."

She whirled on him. "No!"

"Yes."

"You would have forced me?"

"No force would have been necessary."

Heat flooded her cheeks. "I'm not Lady Carlisle or that—I'm not like them."

"No, you're not like them. You're far more alive, and that's where both temptation and pleasure lie. From the beginning you've known what's been between us as well as I have." He looked into her eyes. "You want me as much as I want you."

In the bestselling tradition of Amanda
Quick, a spectacular new historical
romance from the award-winning

Jane Feather

VIXEN

*Chloe Gresham wasn't expecting a warm welcome—
after all her new guardian was a total stranger. But
when Sir Hugo Lattimer strode into Denholm Manor
after a night of carousing and discovered he'd been
saddled with an irrepressible and beautiful young ward,
the handsome bachelor made it perfectly clear he wanted
nothing to do with her. Chloe, however, had ideas of her
own. . . .*

"Come on, lass." Hugo beckoned. "It's bath
time."

Chloe stood her ground, holding on to the back
of the chair, regarding Hugo with the deepest suspicion. "I don't want a bath."

"Oh, you're mistaken, lass. You want a bath
most urgently." He walked toward her with soft-
paced purpose and she backed away.

"What are you going to *do?*"

"Put you under the pump," he said readily,
sweeping her easily into his arms.

"But it's freezing!" Chloe squealed.

"It's a warm night," he observed in reassuring

accents that Chloe didn't find in the least reassuring.

"Put me down. I want to go to bed, Hugo!"

"So you shall . . . so you shall. All in good time." He carried her out to the courtyard. "In fact, we'll *both* go to bed very soon."

Chloe stopped wriggling at that. Despite fatigue and the events of the night, she realized she was far from uninterested in what such a statement might promise.

"Why can't we heat some water and have a proper bath," she suggested carefully.

"It would take too long." He set her down beside the pump, maintaining a hold on her arm. "And it would not convince you of the consequences of headstrong, willful behavior. If you dash into the midst of an inferno, you're going to come out like a chimney sweep." Releasing her arm, he pulled the nightgown over her head so she stood naked in the moonlight.

"And chimney sweeps go under the pump," he declared, working the handle.

A jet of cold water hit her body and Chloe howled. He tossed the soap toward her. "Scrub!"

Chloe thought about dashing out of the freezing jet and into the house, but the filth pouring off her body under the vigorous application of the pump convinced her that she had no choice but to endure this punitive bath. She danced furiously for a few moments, trying to warm herself, then bent to pick up the soap and began to scrub in earnest.

Hugo watched her with amusement and rapidly rising desire. The gyrations of her slender body, silvered in the moonlight, would test the oaths of a monk. She was in such a frantic hurry to get the job over and done with that her movements were devoid of either artifice or invitation, which he found even more arousing.

"I hate you!" she yelled, hurling the soap to the ground. "Stop pumping; I'm clean!"

He released the handle, still laughing. "Such an entrancing spectacle, lass."

"I hate you," she repeated through chattering teeth, bending her head as she wrung the water out of the soaked strands.

"No, you don't." He flung the thick towel around her shoulders. "Rarely have I been treated to such an enticing performance." He began to dry her with rough vigor, rubbing life and warmth into her cold, clean skin.

"I didn't mean to be enticing," she grumbled somewhat halfheartedly, since the compliment was pleasing.

"No, that was part of the appeal," he agreed, turning his attentions to the more intimate parts of her anatomy. "But I trust that in the future you'll think twice before you fling yourself into whatever danger presents itself, my headstrong ward."

Chloe knew perfectly well that given the set of circumstances, she would do the same thing, but it seemed hardly politic or necessary to belabor the issue, particularly when he was doing what he was doing. Warmth was seeping through her in little ripples, and, while her skin was still cold, her heated blood flowed swiftly.

Finally, Hugo dropped the towel and wrapped her in the velvet robe. "Run inside now and pour yourself another tot of rum. You can dry your hair at the range. I'm going to clean myself up."

"Oh?" Chloe raised an eyebrow. "I'm sure it would be easier for you if I worked the pump." She turned up her blistered palms. "I've had a good deal of practice already . . . and besides, I'm entitled to my revenge . . . or do I mean *my* pleasure."

Hugo smiled and stripped off his clothes. "Do your worst, then, lass." He faced her, his body fully aroused, his eyes gleaming with challenge and promise.

With a gleeful chuckle she sent a jet of water over him, careful to circumvent that part of his body that most interested her. Hugo was unperturbed by the cold, having enjoyed many baths under the deck pump of one of His Majesty's ships of the line. The secret was to know it was coming.

With the utmost seriousness he washed himself as she continued to work the handle, but deliberately he offered himself to her wide-eyed gaze. She worked the pump with breathless enthusiasm, her tongue peeping from between her lips, her eyes sparkling with anticipation.

"Enough!" Finally, he held up his hands, demanding surcease. "The show's over. Pass me the towel."

Chloe grinned and continued to work the handle for a few more minutes. Hugo leapt out of the stream and grabbed the damp towel. "You're asking for more trouble, young Chloe." He rubbed his hair and abraded his skin.

"Inside with you, unless you want to go under again." He took a menacing step toward her and with a mock scream she ran into the house, but instead of going to the kitchen she went into Hugo's bedroom, diving beneath the sheets.

When he came in five minutes later, she was lying in his bed, the sheet pulled demurely up to her chin, her cornflower eyes filled with the rich sensuality that never failed to overwhelm him.

"Good morning, Sir Hugo." She kicked off the cover, offering her body, naked, translucent in the pearly dawn light.

"Good morning, my ward." He dropped the towel from his loins and came down on the bed beside her.

ONE FINE DAY

Theresa Weir

The bestselling author of *Last Summer* and *Forever*
offers her most poignant and passionate novel yet.

*After too many years of heartache, Molly Bennet had
packed her bags and run away . . . from her memories,
her husband, and the woman she had become. But just
as she found herself on the brink of a brand-new life, an
unexpected tragedy called her home. Now the man who
had always been so much stronger than Molly needs her
in a way she'd never thought possible. . . .*

"If I touch you . . . you won't run, will you?
Please . . . don't run away."

And there it was again. That ragged catch in
his voice.

And there it was again. Her weakening resolve.
Things were so much easier when you knew who
the enemy was. "No," she whispered. "I won't run."

He reached for her. His fingers touched her
arm, skimming across her skin until he grasped
her hand. He pulled her toward him. She took one
hesitant step, then another.

He lifted her hand . . . and he kissed it. He kissed the chewed nails that were her shame, that she thought so unsightly. His lips touched her palm, her knuckles. Then he pulled in a shaky breath and pressed her hand to the side of his face. She could feel his beard stubble. She could feel the heat of his skin.

And even though she tried to harden herself against him, it did no good. There was no anger left in her. Instead, what she felt was a sweet, unbearable sadness. A sadness that was much worse than anger.

And she found herself wanting to comfort him. She had to fight the urge to wrap her arms around him and pull his head to her breast.

Austin had never stirred such ineffable emotions in her. All her life she'd taken care of the people around her. Sammy . . . Amy . . . But Austin had always been so strong, so invincible. He'd never needed anybody. He'd certainly never needed her.

The limb above their heads creaked. Crickets sang from the deep grass near the edge of the yard.

Austin took both of her hands in his. "Remember that time, shortly after we first met?" he asked. "It was dark. I took you to the park . . . and pushed you in the swing. Do you remember?"

At first she didn't, but then she did. "Yes."

They had laughed together that night. But since then their marriage had contained very little laughter. What had happened to them? she wondered. Where had that kind of joy gone? Why had two such ill-suited people ever gotten married in the first place?

Had there ever been any kind of love between them? Had there ever been a time when their marriage hadn't been so bad?

If nothing else, she had to acknowledge the fact that Austin had given her what Jay couldn't—security.

She could also admit that there had been a brief period of time when they'd gone through the motions of being a family. And in the process, they'd almost become one for real. But it had taken only a carelessly spoken word, a look, to shatter that fragile structure.

"And you . . . sat . . . with me," Austin said.

It was true. She'd forgotten that, too, but now she remembered. She'd sat facing him, a lover's position.

She stood in front of him now, her hands in his. Above them, beyond the leaves, beyond the branches, beyond the jet streams, the stratosphere, and the ionosphere, was what Amy would have called a cartoon moon. Its light wasn't an intrusive light, but merely a hello. A comfort, a candle burning in the window. Beneath it, beneath the shelter of leaves, they were wrapped in the indigo velvet of the night.

He pulled her closer, so they were knee to knee. "It was . . . snowing."

Yes. It *had* been snowing. She'd forgotten that too. And now she remembered how strong his arms had been. How safe he'd made her feel with those arms around her.

Maybe she had almost loved him. Maybe she could have grown to love him, if only things had been different . . .

"I made you . . . wear . . . my coat."

He'd wrapped it around her, thick and warm and scented with the cold.

What had happened to those two people? Where had they gone?

She had no idea what made her do what she did next—she'd never initiated anything between them—but she slipped off her sandals, the grass cool and damp under her bare feet. With both hands on the ropes, she stood facing Austin, knee to knee. He gripped her waist to help steady her as she slid her legs on either side of him, her sundress riding up around her thighs.

His hands moved to her bottom, settling her more firmly against him. Then he grasped the rope, his hands just above hers.

"Ready?" he whispered.

He seemed like the old Austin. The Austin she'd forgotten but now remembered. He was strong, confident, his voice so deep it reverberated against her chest. And yet he was a different Austin too. More mature. More aware. And mixed in with those two people was a stranger, someone she didn't know at all.

Was she ready? "Yes."

And don't miss these spectacular
romances from
Bantam Books, on sale in February:

SILK AND STONE
by **Deborah Smith**
In the compelling tradition of *Blue Willow*,
an enchanting new novel of the heart.

LADY DANGEROUS
by the nationally bestselling author
Suzanne Robinson

SINS OF INNOCENCE
by **Jean Stone**
A poignant novel of four women with only
one thing in common:
each gave her baby to a stranger.

CALL JAN SPILLER'S ASTROLINE

ONLY PERSONALIZED PREDICTIONS!

ONLY FORECAST OF ITS KIND!

This is totally different from any horoscope you've ever heard and is the most authentic astrology forecast available by phone! Gain insight into **LOVE, MONEY, HEALTH, WORK.**

Empower yourself with this amazing astrology forecast. Let our intuitive tarot readings reveal with uncanny insight your personal destiny and the destinies of those close to you.

Jan Spiller, one of the world's leading authorities in astrological prediction, is an AFA Faculty Member, author, full-time astrologer, speaker at astrology and healing conferences, an astrology columnist for national newspapers and magazines, and had her own radio astrology show.

1-900-903-8000 ★ ASTROLOGY FORECAST
1-900-903-9000 ★ TAROT READING

99¢ For The First Min. ★ $1.75 For Each Add'l. Min. ★ Average Length Of Call 7 Min.

CALL NOW AND FIND OUT WHAT THE STARS HAVE IN STORE FOR YOU TODAY!

Call 24 hours a day, 7 days a week. You must be 18 years or older to call and have a touch tone phone. Astral Marketing 1-702-251-1415.

DHS 7/93

OFFICIAL RULES

To enter the sweepstakes below carefully follow all instructions found elsewhere in this offer.

The **Winners Classic** will award prizes with the following approximate maximum values: 1 Grand Prize: $26,500 (or $25,000 cash alternate); 1 First Prize: $3,000; Second Prizes: $400 each; 35 Third Prizes: $100 each; 1,000 Fourth Prizes: $7.50 each. Total maximum retail value of Winners Classic Sweepstakes is $42,500. Some presentations of this sweepstakes may contain individual entry numbers corresponding to one or more of the aforementioned prize levels. To determine the Winners individual entry numbers will first be compared with the winning numbers preselected by computer. For winning numbers not returned, prizes will be awarded in random drawings from among all eligible entries received. Prize choices may be offered at various levels. If a winner chooses an automobile prize, all license and registration fees, taxes, destination charges and, other expenses not offered herein are the responsibility of the winner. If a winner chooses a trip, travel must be complete within one year from the time the prize is awarded. Minors must be accompanied by an adult. Travel companion(s) must also sign release of liability. Trips are subject to space and departure availability. Certain black-out dates may apply.

The following applies to the sweepstakes named above:

No purchase necessary. You can also enter the sweepstakes by sending your name and address to: P.O. Box 508, Gibbstown, N.J. 08027. Mail each entry separately. Sweepstakes begins 6/1/93. Entries must be received by 12/30/94. Not responsible for lost, late, damaged, misdirected, illegible or postage due mail. Mechanically reproduced entries are not eligible. All entries become property of the sponsor and will not be returned.

Prize Selection/Validations: Selection of winners will be conducted no later than 5:00 PM on January 28, 1995, by an independent judging organization whose decisions are final. Random drawings will be held at 1211 Avenue of the Americas, New York, N.Y. 10036. Entrants need not be present to win. Odds of winning are determined by total number of entries received. Circulation of this sweepstakes is estimated not to exceed 200 million. All prizes are guaranteed to be awarded and delivered to winners. Winners will be notified by mail and may be required to complete an affidavit of eligibility and release of liability which must be returned within 14 days of date or notification or alternate winners will be selected in a random drawing. Any prize notification letter or any prize returned to a participating sponsor, Bantam Doubleday Dell Publishing Group, Inc., its participating divisions or subsidiaries, or the independent judging organization as undeliverable will be awarded to an alternate winner. Prizes are not transferable. No substitution for prizes except as offered or as may be necessary due to unavailability, in which case a prize of equal or greater value will be awarded. Prizes will be awarded approximately 90 days after the drawing. All taxes are the sole responsibility of the winners. Entry constitutes permission (except where prohibited by law) to use winners' names, hometowns, and likenesses for publicity purposes without further or other compensation. Prizes won by minors will be awarded in the name of parent or legal guardian.

Participation: Sweepstakes open to residents of the United States and Canada except for the province of Quebec. Sweepstakes sponsored by Bantam Doubleday Dell Publishing Group, Inc., (BDD), 1540 Broadway, New York, NY 10036. Versions of this sweepstakes with different graphics and prize choices will be offered in conjunction with various solicitations or promotions by different subsidiaries and divisions of BDD. Where applicable, winners will have their choice of any prize offered at level won. Employees of BDD, its divisions, subsidiaries, advertising agencies, independent judging organization, and their immediate family members are not eligible.

Canadian residents, in order to win, must first correctly answer a time limited arithmetical skill testing question. Void in Puerto Rico, Quebec and wherever prohibited or restricted by law. Subject to all federal, state, local and provincial laws and regulations. For a list of major prize winners (available after 1/29/95): send a self-addressed, stamped envelope entirely separate from your entry to: Sweepstakes Winners, P.O. Box 517, Gibbstown, NJ 08027. Requests must be received by 12/30/94. DO NOT SEND ANY OTHER CORRESPONDENCE TO THIS P.O. BOX.

SWP 7/93